專欄英語好有趣

吳青樺（Emilia）著

Newspaper Columns with English & Chinese Insights

作者序

　　英語學習，絕對和文化體驗不可分離。大部分的人派上用場和實際驗收英語成果的時候，就是出國旅遊。我一直都在醞釀書寫一本平易近人且貼近生活文化的教學著作，甚至因為要貼近生活面，這本專欄選集我一直避免不小心就做成太像「教科書」或「課本」。

　　記得有一年的秋天，旅遊至日本，那是個網路與智慧型手機都尚未普及的年代，出國仍有找尋網咖的習慣。當我白天探訪了山林間紅葉的美景後，和友人回到東京市區餐廳，享受日本料理的好滋味，用餐席間詢問附近網咖位置，正困擾於日籍服務生無法用英語溝通，打算回到下榻飯店使用商務中心時，幾位服務生竟然在半小時內回到餐桌，遞出一張書寫了滿滿英文的手繪地圖，指示我們如何順利走到網咖。除了驚訝讚嘆日本人服務之用心，內心對於這樣的情況也是充滿衝擊：無法用英語句子交談，卻是有著一定程度的英文字彙量，足夠寫出所有道路標示等字彙！為什麼背了許多英文字，但沒有辦法「講出英文」？沒有辦法順利「聽懂英文」？這個現象也是我觀察不少學生從小到大學習英語仍會面臨的窘境，應付完了考試，有「認識英語」？「使用英語」？「喜歡英語文化」嗎？

　　四年前開始有稿件邀約撰寫工商時報每週六的英語教學專欄，每週的靈感都是日常生活以及新聞新知。教學相長，在累積了各處教學和企業訓練經驗後，與學生的互動更是我滿滿的寫作來源，每一回學生的發問都讓我更曉得要如何補強教學，感謝過往的每位學生，你們都是我可貴的老師！此外也要感謝當年邀稿專欄的世界文化中心總編輯Emi Lee，因著這個機會，開始每週和大家分享英語新知。還要感謝周遭親朋好友，這之中有許多各行各業的專業，讓我從生活大小事汲取了滿滿的寫作內容，轉化成一篇篇根據真實故事啟發的英文專欄，讓這本書「生活化」又「實在」。還有萬分感謝暢銷書作者兼大學講師Sean L.的牽線與

推薦，不只促成這段與瑞蘭國際合作的開始，還身兼我的文章靈感來源之一。以下各領域友人也是我的文章真實靈感來源，本書收錄了各至少一篇他們啟發我的專欄：感謝美國籍瑜伽名師Angela的樂活生活態度。感謝Ryan和Brenda的食品安全知識。感謝Christina在美容時尚領域對我專欄的影響。感謝美國東岸友人Zoe和Ethan，我們一起看完百老匯音樂劇，一路哼著歌回家的情景仍歷歷在目。感謝西雅圖友人Julianne的招待以及在當地分享生活。感謝澳洲法籍友人和我分享澳洲主要城市文化活動和慶典。特別感謝我的超級啦啦隊，英國籍工程師Bruce Philp協助閱讀稿件的英文內容，我們一同確認了專欄裡的科技業辭彙，以及英式英語和美式英語的道地用字。感謝瑞蘭國際專業且優秀的編輯團隊。你們都是我最好的老師，我何其感恩。

誠摯地和大家分享這本生活化又實用有趣的作品。期待大家培養英語思維看世界，並愛上英語學習、享受英語學習。

吳青樺 Emilen W.

推薦序

　　好書值得等待，Emilia老師的新書終於問世了！我和Emilia老師的初認識，恰巧就是在她開始撰寫工商時報英語教學專欄時。過去這四年來，看著她完成了一篇篇實用、生活化、且生動有趣的專欄，內容有Emilia老師翻譯寫作的功力和長期觀察英語新聞報導的專業，可說是非常有深度，精彩萬分。

　　教學相長，身為大學講師和作者，我深刻了解這個道理：一本語言書的寫作必須搭配教學經歷，把實際教學的經驗融入書本中，才有辦法傳遞真正有用的知識。我一直帶著這樣專業的熱忱砥礪自己的教學，也時常和Emilia老師互相鼓勵與分享。因為夠專業、持續進修求知，才能讓語言教學不被時代淘汰。

　　Emilia老師多年的教學裡，生動活潑的講課風格一直深受學生喜愛，上課時經常補充英語新知、流行用語、新聞字彙，也擅於用有系統的方法矯正學生的發音，並用文化觀點訓練企業界學生使用英語交談。這本書的出版，讓你即使沒有機會上Emilia老師的課，也能搭配隨書附贈的MP3，實際獲得臨場學習的感受與感動。也很感謝Emilia老師的努力，讓好的教學能更普及，也讓有需要的學生們，在能負擔的價位，就能得到用心的教學。

　　如同我上課時告訴學生們：「學習一種語言，同時也是在學習它的文化。兩者不可能分開，亦是相輔相成。」期望更多讀者和學生在英語學習上建立興趣，進而學習道地的英語。就讓這本《專欄英語好有趣》幫助你更認識英語文化，輕鬆並有系統地學會各領域的英語和知識。

國立臺北科技大學 講師

博客來、金石堂 第一名暢銷書《72小時5000單》作者

林尚禮 Sean Li

本書介紹

　　本書節錄了作者過去四年刊登於工商時報週六副刊的英語教學專欄，並在書目各單元增添了當初報紙上沒有的衍生英語用語、相關英語辭彙、文化背景知識、生活照片，且搭配詳盡的實用英語例句和情境對話練習，就是為了幫助讀者學習更有深度的道地英語。

　　作者秉持語言學習的宗旨不該離開文化歷史與日常生活新知，集結了八大主題的中英語專欄，運用本人實際在大專院校與留學機構教學、企業外派訓練的專業，和在業界翻譯與寫作的經驗，然後和讀者分享如何學習生活文化面的新聞英語。

　　本書英語學習內容包羅萬象，從食衣住行主題到各行各業用語都有，並且維持報紙專欄的特色，介紹英語世界新知以及歷史新聞。此外，全書也特別針對上班族口語會話和社會新鮮人求職的英語加以著墨，以期增強讀者的會話能力。相信只要搭配隨書所附的光碟閱讀與練習，就能更加認識英語文化，帶起英語學習的興趣、掌握正確的學習方法，一起享受英語、愛上英語。

吳青樺 Emilon W.

如何使用本書

為了讓每個翻開《專欄英語好有趣》的讀者，都能持續保持學習動力，本書在內容以及編排上都下足苦心，帶你從生活文化面切入，從此不再害怕新聞英語、重新認識新聞英語、愛上新聞英語！並同步培養聽說讀寫4大能力，和外國人交談不再找不到話題！

全書8大主題，橫跨最多領域

本書分為8大主題，廣泛收錄「日常生活大小事」、「生活風尚潮流」、「餐飲英語」、「辦公室現象」、「科技革新」、「商業經濟」、「新聞報導與當代議題」、「履歷求職大作戰」等各類英語專欄，包含不同元素，給你最豐富多元的英語題材，攝取不同面向的新知。

作者導讀＋外師標準發音MP3，學習英語不受限

作者為每篇專欄親自錄製生動活潑的導讀MP3，讓你即使沒時間看書，也能邊聽邊學；而情境對話則由作者與外籍名師共同示範標準英語發音，讓你正確學習英語發音及外國人說話的音調。

全書專欄中的英語敘述，都有中文的同步對照，有任何看不懂的地方，可以迅速參考中文，不因排斥全英語而降低學習英語的意願，拉近你和英語之間的距離。

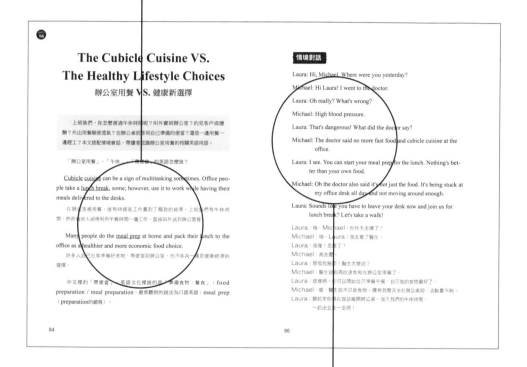

16

The Cubicle Cuisine VS.
The Healthy Lifestyle Choices
辦公室用餐 VS. 健康新選擇

上班族們，你怎麼度過午休時間呢？叫外賣到辦公室？約見客戶或應酬？外出用餐順便透氣？在辦公桌前享用自己準備的便當？還是一邊趕工？本文搭配情境會話，帶讀者認識辦公室用餐的相關英語用語。

「辦公室用餐」、「午休」、「帶便當」的英語怎麼說？

Cubicle cuisine can be a sign of multitasking sometimes. Office people take a lunch break, some; however, use it to work while having their meals delivered to the desks.

在辦公室裡用餐，還有時候是工作量到了極致的結果。上班族們有午休時間，然而有些人卻用午餐時間一邊工作，直接叫外送到辦公室裡。

Many people do the meal prep at home and pack their lunch to the office as a healthier and more economic food choice.

許多人自己在家準備好食物，帶便當到辦公室，也不失為一種更健康經濟的選擇。

中文裡的「帶便當」（在英語文化裡說的是「準備食物、餐食」；food preparation / meal preparation，最常聽到的說法為口語英語：meal prep（preparation的縮寫）。

84

情境對話

Laura: Hi, Michael. Where were you yesterday?

Michael: Hi Laura! I went to the doctor.

Laura: Oh really? What's wrong?

Michael: High blood pressure.

Laura: That's dangerous! What did the doctor say?

Michael: The doctor said no more fast food and cubicle cuisine at the office.

Laura: I see. You can start your meal prep for the lunch. Nothing's better than your own food.

Michael: Oh the doctor also said it's not just the food. It's being stuck at my office desk all day and not moving around enough.

Laura: Sounds like you have to leave your desk now and join us for lunch break? Let's take a walk!

Laura：嗨，Michael，你昨天去哪了？
Michael：嗨，Laura！我去看了醫生。
Laura：是喔！怎麼了？
Michael：高血壓。
Laura：那很危險耶！醫生怎麼說？
Michael：醫生說別再吃速食和在辦公室用餐了。
Laura：這樣啊，你可以開始自己準備午餐，自己做的食物最好了。
Michael：喔，醫生還說不只是食物，還有我整天坐在辦公桌前，活動量不夠。
Laura：聽起來你現在就該離開辦公桌，加入我們的午休時間。
一起出去走一走吧！

86

在生活相關的主題分類中，適時加入了模擬情境對話，除了讓內容更加活潑，讓你也能透過對話，學習口語英語。

焦點英語，非學不可的精華

焦點英語只揀選出2至3個重點關鍵字，再提供音標、詞性、中文解釋、例句等資訊，份量精簡，學習完全沒有負擔！

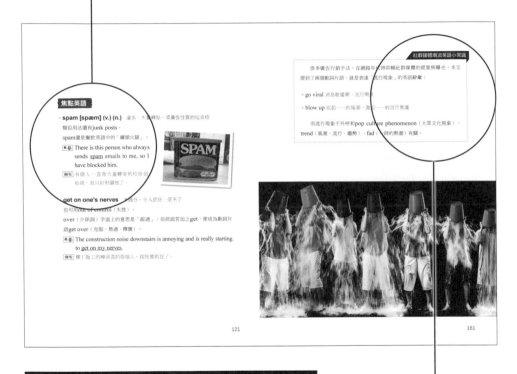

焦點英語

· spam [spæm] (v.) (n.) 灌水　大量轉貼，或廣告性質的垃圾信
類似用法還有junk posts。
spam還是餐飲英語中的「罐頭火腿」。

e.g. There is this person who always sends spam emails to me, so I have blocked him.

例句 有個人一直寄大量轉寄的垃圾信給我，我只好封鎖他了。

get on one's nerves 過分、令人抓狂、受不了
也可用out of control（失控）。
over（介係詞）字面上的意思是「超過」，但前面若加上get，便成為動詞片語get over（克服、熬過、釋懷）。

e.g. The construction noise downstairs is annoying and is really starting to get on my nerves.

例句 樓下施工的噪音真的很煩人，我快要抓狂了。

社群媒體潮流英語小常識

很多廣告行銷手法，在網路年代得仰賴社群媒體的經營與曝光。本文提到了兩個動詞片語，就是表達「流行現象」的英語辭彙：

· go viral 消息散播開、流行開來

· blow up 吹起……的風潮、激起……的流行意識

而流行現象不外乎和pop culture phenomenon（大眾文化現象）、trend（風潮、流行、趨勢）、fad（一時的熱潮）有關。

121

161

英語小常識、衍生用語，補充語言文化資訊

補充關鍵字的同義用法、詞語來源、衍生用語等語言文化的相關資料，不僅常保新鮮感，想要增進額外知識的你，也可以善加利用！

目 錄

Chapter 1   Everyday English   15
日常生活大小事

| **Chapter 2** | **Lifestyles and Fashion** 生活風尚潮流 | **39** |

**Chapter
5**

Technology and Innovations   **117**
科技革新

Chapter 1

Everyday English
日常生活大小事

Your Everyday Conversations: "How's the Weather?"

如何開啟聊天話題？生活化的天氣用語

英語社交場合中，打招呼寒暄之後，接下來該聊些什麼？怎麼聊才不會冷場？本文示範口語對話中最常被聊到的主題：天氣，帶讀者來認識更生活化的英語交談。

以下4段情境對話，用天氣當聊天的開場白，再帶出更多互動！一起學習如何用英語真正交談、製造話題，並拉近人際關係。讓你用英語談論天氣時，不再只停留在「今天天氣如何？」（What's the weather like today? / How's the weather?）。

情境對話

Edward: What's the weather <u>forecast</u> for the rest of the week?

Tina: It says we will have blue skies this week!

Edward: Good to hear that! Hey, let's go out on the coming weekend!

Edward：接下來一週的氣象預報怎麼說？
Tina：整週都是晴朗的好天氣喔！
Edward：真開心聽到是這樣！嘿！這週末我們出去吧！

Edward: Do you have rain there?

Tina: It hasn't been raining for many weeks.

Edward: Oh I see! Is it normal in this season?

Tina: No idea. Actually I love it when it's not rainy.

Edward：你們那邊有下雨嗎？
Tina：這邊已經好幾週沒下雨了。
Edward：喔，這樣子啊！這季節這樣算正常的嗎？
Tina：不曉得耶。其實我愛沒下雨的時候。

Edward: What's the temperature in Taipei?

Tina: It is 15 degree Celsius today, which is a lot warmer than before.

Edward: Sounds great!

Tina: Yes, indeed!

Edward：台北溫度幾度？
Tina：今天有（攝氏）15度，比之前溫暖多了。
Edward：聽起來太棒了！
Tina：對呀，沒錯！

Edward: Is it a beautiful day for a walk?

Tina: We couldn't ask for a better day!

Edward: Let's take a walk through the park!

Tina: Good idea! I'm in!

Edward：今天這樣美麗的天氣很適合散步吧？
Tina：找不到更適合的日子囉！（擇日不如撞日！）
Edward：去公園散散步吧！
Tina：好主意！我要加入！

焦點英語

· **forecast ['for͵kæst] (n.) (v.)** 預報、預測

以fore為字首的英文字，有「事先、先前」的意思，同before。

e.g. Those are today's headlines. Next, our weather man, Larry, will give us the weather <u>forecast</u> for the rest of the week.

例句 這些是今天的頭條新聞。接下來，我們的氣象主播——賴瑞，將為我們報導本週接下來的天氣預報。

· **normal ['nɔrm!] (adj.)** 正常

反義詞abnormal

e.g. In <u>normal</u> circumstances, he wouldn't sign the contracts without reviewing for a couple of days.

例句 在正常情況下，他會把合約反覆讀幾天再簽名。

· **temperature ['tɛmprətʃɚ] (n.)** 溫度

e.g. The doctor said the patient's body <u>temperature</u> was back to the normal, but he still had to stay in the hospital for observation.

例句 醫生說病患的體溫已回復正常，但仍須住院觀察。

衍生氣溫單字

本文中描述天氣溫度的口語對話，可用「it's + adj.」的句型，搭配以下依照氣溫高低標示的溫度形容詞。

· **It's hot.**　　　　炎熱

· **It's warm.**　　　溫暖

· **It's cool.**　　　　涼爽

· **It's cold.**　　　　冷

· **It's freezing.**　　嚴寒、超冷的

warm、cool為最舒適（comfortable）的氣溫。

Are You Getting a Cold or Just Seasonal Allergies?

換季過敏？感冒？英語傻傻分不清？

季節交替的時節裡，你換季過敏了嗎？還是日夜溫差讓你傷風感冒了？該怎麼用英語敘述這些影響或輕或重的症狀？本文帶讀者來看看過敏症狀和感冒的英語詞彙和情境例句。

Is it a cold or seasonal <u>allergies</u>?

到底是感冒了還是換季過敏？

英語裡常用複數，因為通常過敏會伴隨多種不同症狀（symptoms）。換季過敏有時會讓人誤以為是感冒了，來看看以下敘述和比較：

It's springtime, and as if on cue, your nose starts to run, your eyes are puffy and watery, and you suddenly sneeze several times a day. Is it a cold or do you have a seasonal allergy?

春天到了，一切好像說好的一樣，你的鼻子開始流鼻水、眼睛老是水汪汪的又腫又癢，然後突然間，一整天不斷打噴嚏！到底是感冒了還是換季過敏？

看看下面表格的比較，查驗你是感冒還是過敏？

Colds 感冒

· Symptoms often <u>appear</u> one at a time: first sneezing,
then a runny nose, then congestion.

通常症狀是一個接一個發生：先打噴嚏、接著流鼻水、然後鼻塞。

· Generally last from seven to ten days.

普遍會持續7到10天。

· May be accompanied by a fever.

可能伴隨發燒。

Allergies 過敏

· Symptoms <u>occur</u> all at once.

症狀一口氣全部來。

· Continue as long as a person is exposed to the allergy-causing agent
(<u>allergen</u>).

只要置身於過敏原中，症狀就會持續發生。

· Not usually associated with a fever.

通常不會發燒。

· **allergy ['ælɚdʒi] (n.)**　過敏

e.g. My skin <u>allergy</u> got worse as the rainy season came.

例句 我皮膚過敏在雨季來時變得更嚴重了。

· **appear [ə'pɪr] (v.)**　顯露、出現、發生、似乎

e.g. He <u>appeared</u> to be talking to himself.

例句 他似乎在自言自語。

· **occur [ə'kɚ] (v.)**　引發、發生、浮現、存在

e.g. Earthquakes <u>occur</u> frequently in this area.

例句 這一地區經常發生地震。

· **allergen ['ælədʒən] (n.)**　過敏原

更口語的講法為allergy-causing agent。

e.g. Cockroach is one of the major sources of <u>allergens</u>.

例句 蟑螂為主要過敏原中的一種。

流感英語小常識

　　比傷風感冒（cold）更糟糕的，就是患上流行性感冒了！流行性感冒和單純小感冒的英語講法不一樣：「come down with the flu」。

e.g. I went to the doctor yesterday, and he said I <u>came down with the flu</u> and had to take a day off to get some more rest.

例句 我昨晚看了醫生，醫生說我得的是流感，必須請假一天多休息。

Healthier Choices: Why Is It Important to Exercise in the Cold Weather?

健康生活自己選：冷天運動好處多

濕冷的冬天讓你更不想運動嗎？本文列舉冷天運動的好處，讓讀者兼顧健康之餘，也學習相關英語用語。

Many of us tend to think that winter is a great time to relax and skip sports. However, there are six reasons why it's crucial to work out in the cold weather.

許多人冬天就偷懶不運動，然而，以下6個理由將會讓你改觀，發現冷天裡運動的好處。

- **Burn excess calories.**
  燃燒多餘的卡路里。

We consume more "comfort food" in this holiday season. Prevent winter weight and get ready for the summer faster by exercising regularly in the winter.

冬天裡的年假讓我們不小心吃了更多「療癒美食」。這就是冬天更需要運動來擺脫體脂肪的原因，提早準備迎接夏天的體態。

- **Improve the immune system.**
  增強免疫力。

  Regular workout helps reduce the risk of colds and the flu, especially in the cold weather.

  規律的健身絕對可以降低傷風感冒的機率，特別在天氣冷的時候。

- **Improve your mood.**
  改善心情。

  Studies show that exercise helps boost your "feel-good" <u>endorphin</u>, which means making you happier. This is something to defeat the winter blues.

  研究顯示，運動可幫助刺激分泌讓人感覺良好的腦內啡，也就是說，運動讓你更開心。腦內啡絕對可以幫你戰勝冬季的憂鬱。

- **Break a habit of making excuses.**
  戒除找理由的壞習慣。

  Why not break this habit now this winter? It's challenging, but you will develop a new habit of exercising regularly no matter what.

  不如趁這個冬天戒掉這習慣吧？有點困難，但你會因此而有機會培養規律運動的新習慣。

- **Learn how to exercise in unpredictable situation.**
  學習不論在什麼處境下都可運動。

Cold weather is always full of surprises. Be creative and active even staying indoors by doing yoga for example. Think about some winter sports outside as well.

寒冷的天氣當然讓活動的安排充滿變數，不過你可以發揮創意想想室內的運動，例如瑜伽。也剛好可以想想適合冬季的戶外運動。

- **Live a longer life.**
  更長壽。

An active life is the key to a longer life for sure.

這點不用多說，要活就要動，這絕對是維持長壽的關鍵。

焦點英語

- **endorphin [en'dɔ:rfɪn] (n.)** 　內啡肽，亦稱腦內啡或安多酚

  e.g. An <u>endorphin</u> is a chemical produced by your body that reduces pain and can make you feel happier.

  例句 腦內啡是身體裡的一種化學物質，能減輕疼痛，並可讓人感覺較開心。

A Bad Hair Day?!

三千煩惱絲讓你抓狂嗎？諸事不順的英語怎麼說？

　　某國際時尚雜誌曾統計並分析各國女性最在意的外觀部分，亞洲女性追求白皙無暇的肌膚（fair skin）；北美洲女性則是對於髮型有相當程度的偏執！

　　相信很多女人都熟知，特別潮溼、或者是刮大風又過分乾燥的氣候會破壞髮型美觀，且影響髮質。不過，當美國人說「I had a bad hair day!」可不一定在抱怨他的髮型有多糟多亂喔！頂著一頭讓人不滿意、又無精打采的亂髮出門見人，的確會讓人心情不佳，甚至影響一整天的辦事效率！於是口語中衍生出了這個和頭髮相關的俚語，來形容「諸事不順的一天」！

　　根據美國方言協會（American Dialect Society）的研究記載，第一次出現「a bad hair day」這個俚語用法，是在1988年休士頓記事報（Houston Chronicle）的一篇專欄，文中描述不順利的倒楣經歷，在那天給當事者帶來嚴重的影響和沮喪的心情。

　　來看看以下的情境例句：

I had a bad hair day! First, my computer shut down this morning. And then, I forgot an important meeting with my clients. I came home with bad hair.

今天真是諸事不順！一開始是早上電腦當機，接下來我又忘了和客戶有個重要的會議。最後心煩意亂地回到家。

原來，a bad hair day形容a day when everything seems to go wrong!
（這天什麼事都不順），也可以用「It's not my day!」來表達同樣沮喪的感受。

當然，這個俚語也是可以用來描述真的是因為髮型不佳，而影響到一整天心情的，來看看下面兩種情況的例句：

I woke up this morning, and then I thought, today, it is going to be terrible because of my messy hair. I know I sound like I'm having a bad hair day. But nothing seems to be working out. As for my hair, what a mess!

今早醒來時，光是看到我那頭整理不好的亂
髮，我就有預感今天會很倒楣。聽起來好像
我今天真的是諸事不順，但的確似乎
沒有一件事順利。至於我的頭
髮，糟透了！

Is she having a bad hair day or what? I've never seen hair that color before! I don't mean to <u>pick on her</u>, but I've never met anyone who can <u>get on my nerves</u> like her!

她頭髮是怎麼了？可以再糟一點！我從來沒有看過誰的頭髮是那種顏色的！我無意在背後這樣說她，可是我還真的沒遇過誰可以讓我這樣受不了的！

剪壞的髮型讓你抓狂了嗎？或是換季時的多雨潮溼天氣，讓你難以整理頭髮，而影響到心情了嗎？下回聽到人家說「I had a bad hair day!」可別先急著安慰對方的髮型，要適時展現關心、表現同理心（empathy），示意對方你理解他／她倒楣的心情！

焦點英語

· **pick on someone** （故意）針對某人挑毛病或找麻煩

同義詞 get on one's case

e.g. Dave, can you please be a dear and stop <u>picking on</u> your baby sister?

例句 Dave，可不可以拜託你行行好，別再找你小妹麻煩了？

· **get on one's nerves** 令人抓狂

e.g. It's difficult to get a taxicab during the rush hour, and this really <u>getting on my nerves</u> before my meeting.

例句 交通尖峰時刻超難叫到計程車，讓我在開會前要抓狂了。

　　渡過了壓力更大、更不順的一天嗎？上述I had a bad hair day或It's not my day today都還不足以形容你的感受嗎？英語人士還有更誇張的說法：pull the hair out / pull someone's hair out，用來表達不順心到想把頭髮一把給扯掉的感受！來看看這句模擬拍片劇組人員的對戲心得：

"Usually the table read went really well, but sometimes you just had a pull-your-hair-out day going through the play script!"

「通常大家坐下來一桌對台詞時都進展得很好，但有時候在順劇本還是會不順利到讓你想一把把頭髮給扯了！」

Rush Hour:
Hail a Cab Or Take a Taxi?

尖峰時間，計程車都去哪裡了？

你有這樣的經驗嗎？交通尖峰時間趕搭計程車，卻等不到一台空車，或是好不容易搭上了計程車，卻因塞車讓你在車內乾著急，看著錶直跳。本文是作者在紐約的親自觀察，帶讀者以英語觀點看看紐約市計程車現象，學習怎麼用英語說「招計程車」、「跳錶」等相關大都會交通用語。

Ever feel as if you can't get a <u>cab</u> in the rush hour?

曾經有這樣的感覺嗎？交通尖峰時間招不到計程車？

例句中的用的cab是什麼講法？cab一詞，是典型美國人、尤其是紐約客的道地講法，意思就是「計程車」。當然，你也可以用taxi、taxicab。

而「招計程車」的英語要怎麼說呢？動詞可以用hail或更口語的get，所以hail a cab、get a cab、hail a taxi、get a taxicab這幾種講法都通。

來從下面幾句描述紐約市中心曼哈頓計程車現象的例句學習英語：

New data have confirmed the perception that just as afternoon rush is beginning; the taxicabs disappear by the hundreds. Many are heading from Manhattan to Queens for a <u>shift change</u>.

新的觀察數據證實了紐約市的計程車現象：午後尖峰時刻之前，計程車車潮大幅減少了上百輛，許多計程車都從曼哈頓（市中心）開往皇后區（市郊）輪班。

The number of cabs that pick up at least two <u>fares</u> from 4 to 5 p.m. is the lowest of any hour between 7 a.m. and midnight, the data show.

數據顯示，紐約計程車開始載客的上午7點到午夜，下午4點到5點間，有載客、且車資跳錶至少2次的計程車數量是一天中最低的。

In Manhattan, the hour from 4 to 5 p.m. has long been considered a low tide of taxi service, the maddening moment when entire fleets of empty yellow cabs flip on their <u>off-duty lights</u> and proceed past the office workers seeking a way home.

一直以來，下午4點到5點間是曼哈頓計程車服務最不發達的時候。這段讓人抓狂的時間中，想招車回家的上班族眼睜睜看著黃色車潮呼嘯而過，明明有空車，卻因為計程車輪班時間而不載客。

◀作者於2012年10月，在紐約曼哈頓街頭的麥迪遜廣場（Madison Square）外招計程車，卻巧遇計程車排班輪調，而遲遲等不到可載客的空車。

· **shift change** （交通車輛）輪班；（排班人員）班表輪值

e.g. All the buses and the drivers are at the terminal station for a <u>shift change</u>.

例句 所有巴士和司機都在客運總站排輪班。

· **fare [fɛr]** （計程車跳錶）車資

e.g. Do you know the taxi <u>fare</u> for one pickup from the airport to the office?

例句 從機場去辦公室，你知道單趟計程車車資多少嗎？

· **off-duty lights** 計程車（顯示空車但休息或遇到輪班）不載客

e.g. I wonder why there are so many taxicabs in downtown with <u>off-duty lights</u> on. I can't get a taxi to go to the meeting!

例句 不曉得市中心怎麼會那麼多計程車休息不載客，我招不到車去開會！

British VS. American English
英美用語大不同

英式英語和美式英語除了口音和一些字詞拼法的不同外，還有許多詞彙講法的差異，反應了兩邊文化著眼點的不同，正如台灣和中國大陸一樣，兩邊有許多不同的中文講法。本文將帶讀者了解幾種日常生活英語裡，英美的不同講法。

American began to change the sound of their speech after the Revolutionary War in 1776. They wanted to separate themselves from the British.

美國人自從脫離大英帝國獨立後，為了和英國人有所區別，自1776年戰後開始改變他們的英語語音。

· 公寓：美 **apartment** 英 **flat**
美式英語中的flat是指「整層或一層一戶的大樓住家」。連帶「室友」的講法也有不同：美 roommate 英 flat mate

· 電梯：美 **elevator** 英 **lift**

· 人行道：美 **sidewalk** 英 **pavement**

· 長褲：美 **pants** 英 **trousers**

· 中場休息：美 **intermission** 英 **interval**

· 擋風玻璃：美 **windshield** 英 **windscreen**

· 水龍頭：美 **faucet** 英 **tap**

· 卡車：美 **truck** 英 **lorry**

· 戲院：美 **theater** 英 **theatre**

發音相同，美國獨立建國後，韋式字典（Merriam-Webster's Dictionary）依據發音而更改了美式拼法。類似例子還有「灰色」，美式英語是gray，英式英語是grey。

· 介係詞用法不同的例子：

While the British would go out "at the weekend", Americans would go out "on the weekend." While the British would play "in a team", Americans would play "on a team."

週末出門，英式英語的介係詞用「"at" the weekend」，美式英語則是「"on" the weekend」。球隊或運動團隊裡，英式英語用「"in" a team」，美式英語是「"on" a team」。

· 地鐵：美 **subway** 英 **underground**

倫敦是全世界第一個擁有地下鐵的城市，當年對英國人而言，其概念猶如下水道或地下管線，所以除了underground，倫敦人也暱稱地鐵為tube（管子），一直沿用至今。

· 汽油：美 **gas (gasoline)** 英 **petrol (petroleum)**

· 圓環：美 **traffic circle** 英 **roundabout**

· 十字路口：美 **intersection** 英 **junction / crossroads**

· 廁所（俚語）：美 **John** 英 **loo**

· 毛衣：美 **sweater** 英 **jumper**

· 運動鞋（健身房用）：美 **gym shoes** 英 **trainers**

這邊講的是特別帶去健身房的運動鞋，有趣的是，健身房裡的器材教練，美式英語是trainer。

· 浴袍：美 **bathrobe** 英 **dressing gown**

· 郵遞區號：美 **zip code** 英 **post code**

· 足球：美 **soccer** 英 **football**

若是特別提到美式足球（橄欖球），美國人講football，因此英式英語講美式足球時，便說American football。

· 不客氣：美 **You're welcome.** 英 **Not at all.**

Generally, it is agreed that no one version is "correct". However, these are certainly preferences in use.

大致上來說，不管是美式還是英式，英語人士也同意，沒有哪一種講法才正確。只是表現出兩邊英語的用法偏好不同而已。

...s were the first form of mass transportation and had an effective monopoly on land transport until the development...
...otorcar in the early 20th century. Railway companies in Europe and the United States used streamlined tra...
...33 for high-speed services with an average speed of up to 130 km/h (80 mph) and a top speed of more than...
...00 mph). The first high-speed train was the Italian ETR 200 that in July 1939 went from Milan to Florence at...
...ith a top speed of 203 km/h. With this service, these trains were able to compete with the upcoming airplan...
..., the Odakyu Electric Railway in Greater Tokyo launched its Romancecar 3000 SSE. This set a world record...
...gauge trains at 145 km/h (90 mph), giving Japanese designers confidence that they could safely build even fa...

Chapter 2

Lifestyles and Fashion
生活風尚潮流

Fast Fashion: Masstige

大眾愛平價好貨！

　　平價時尚的話題近幾年席捲全台，除了知名歐美日品牌終於來台設櫃之外，許多平價時尚品牌讓伸展台（runway）上的流行已遠低於國際精品大牌的價格，快速陳列於賣場，提供了消費者更經濟的選擇。來看看大眾喜愛的平價好貨，英語怎麼說。

· **masstige**　平價時尚單品

字典裡查無此字，masstige是mass（大眾）和prestige（名聲、高級品質）2字組合成的新詞，是市場行銷用語（marketing term）中所謂的平價高級貨，介於「大量生產的低價位商品」與「有品牌的高價位商品」之間。

e.g. Now I'm a married woman with little mouths to feed. I can't afford such luxuries like the certain brand I used to spend a fortune on. For now, <u>masstige</u> products are good enough for me.

例句 結婚後，家裡有小孩要養，再也買不起這種一擲千金的貴婦保養品了。現在，平價又好用的產品就夠了。

· **off-the-shelf products**　開架產品

shelf是賣場中的商品陳列架，off the shelf是指「可立即從庫存中出售，且現成、不用訂製」。

e.g. Joseph: Your skin is radiant and fair. What have you been using?
Bella: Just the usual <u>off-the-shelf products</u>.
Joseph: Are they reliable?
Bella: I suppose so. They work fine for me.

對話 Joseph：你的皮膚看起來亮白無暇！最近用了什麼保養品？

Bella：只是一般的開架品而已。

Joseph：那些可靠嗎？

Bella：應該吧。我用了有效果。

· **fast fashion** 平價時尚

如同近幾年來台灣設櫃的風潮，fast fashion是時尚業（fashion industry）用語，即「流行、時尚、快速、平價的服飾」。

e.g. Fast-fashion purveyors make their millions by knocking off runway designs and marketing them to the masses.

例句 快速將伸展台上的高級訂製服以更低的價位打入大眾市場中，平價流行的承辦商以此賺進了大把的鈔票。

Social Media Posting: "Throwback Thursday"

社群網站新趨勢：每週四流行什麼？

近幾年社群網路越趨成熟、普及，也發展出幾種張貼文章的流行趨勢。本文帶讀者來認識Facebook、Twitter、Tumblr、Instagram上流行的英語關鍵字，以及相關的網路文化、用語。

#TBT和#throwbackthursday，這2個常在Instagram歐美帳號看到的英語搜尋標籤（hashtag），到底是什麼網路關鍵字？

經常使用Facebook、Twitter、Tumblr、Instagram的讀者，對上面2個hashtag（關鍵字搜尋標籤）一定不陌生，但到底什麼是throw back？發文內容或發布的照片又該是什麼主題呢？

It's a weekly social media posting theme that on Thursdays anyone can participate in the "Throwback Thursday" trend by posting content, usually photos, to remember a past event.

英語世界裡的社群網站，每週四流行張貼這種主題的內容（通常是照片）來回味過往。

原來throw back這個片語是「回顧、懷舊」的意思。

Why is "Throwback Thursday" so popular? Social media is used for sharing our lives, and people love the feeling of <u>nostalgia</u> in addition to what is happening.

為何這種「懷舊週四」的主題（在英語世界）如此受歡迎？人們使用社群網路來分享生活，而分享當下之外，大家還喜愛懷舊的感覺。

There's an interesting fact that businesses and brands have also begun using the "TBT" theme as a part of the social media marketing strategies.

從商業面來看，有趣的事實是，商人和各大廠牌已經開始以縮寫為TBT的「懷舊週四」關鍵字為主題，當作網路行銷的策略之一。

典型「懷舊週四」的張貼內容可能有以下的文字敘述再搭配一張老照片：

這個網路社群的週四趨勢已經發展成了小遊戲，甚至發文者可能意猶未盡，而衍生出以下的英語搜尋標籤：#flashbackfriday（回顧週五），繼續發布過往的回憶。

現學現賣這幾個英語關鍵字，這週四、週五你有什麼老照片想張貼出來分享呢？小提醒，別忘了搜尋標籤（hashtag）的「#」後面，文字不用空格，才能順利讓你發文的相關內容被搜尋到喔！

· **throw back**　回顧、懷舊、緬懷

　e.g.　Getting old means sometimes you would <u>throw back</u> to the good old days.

　例句　年紀越長，代表有時你會回顧過往美好的時光。

· **nostalgia [nɑsˈtældʒɪə] (n.)**　鄉愁、思鄉、念舊感

　e.g.　Strolling down the small town and having the street food gave him a feeling of <u>nostalgia</u> thinking of his childhood memory here.

　例句　在小鎮閒逛，一邊吃著路邊小吃，讓他感到一陣鄉愁，想起了孩提時代在這裡的回憶

· **flash back**　（如幻燈片一幕幕地）回顧過往、回憶、想當年、懷舊、懷古

　e.g.　Seeing the old photo book at his grandmother's made him <u>flash back</u> to the family time there.

　例句　看到祖母家的老相本，讓他回憶起一幕幕家人在這裡團聚的時光。

Party Cultures:
Don't Be a Party Crash!

英語世界派對文化

英語世界的派對文化和其禮節，你都知道嗎？本文帶讀者認識不同形式的家庭聚會派對和英語用語，並輔以情境對話幫助你學習英語。

Crashing a party is viewed as the act of attending to a party when not invited or not welcomed.

派對中不請自來、或不受歡迎的人士，會被看做是去砸場的！

crash a party 意思就是「砸場、鬧場」。受邀前往派對前，總要顧到禮節和文化習俗，來瞭解以下幾種常見的家庭派對（home party / house party）：

· **potluck**

a gathering of people where everyone brings a dish.

每人準備、帶一道菜的派對形式。

· **baby shower**

a celebration of the pending or the recent birth of a baby by presenting gifts to the parents.

為了即將出生、或剛出生的寶寶而舉辦，客人在此派對上送禮給寶寶的父母、以示祝賀。

· **dinner party** 晚宴、晚餐聚會。

- **welcome party** 接風、歡迎會。

- **farewell party / say-goodbye party** 餞行、歡送會。

- **class reunion** 同學會。

- **tea party** 茶會。

- **bachelor's party / bacherlorette's party**
  婚前單身派對，分男女個別舉辦。還有為了準新娘（bride-to-be）舉辦的gift-giving party（bridal shower），出席者贈送禮物給準新娘，以示祝福。

- **housewarming** 喬遷、新居落成派對。

- **cocktail party** 雞尾酒派對。

- **ugly sweater party**
  a party where everyone is required to wear a hideous holiday sweater, usually during the Christmas season.
  通常在聖誕假期舉辦的醜毛衣派對，大家都得穿上最可笑的毛衣出席，以表示冬季的節慶氣氛。

- **birthday party / surprise party** 生日／驚喜派對。

Edward: I've just received the invitation to the party.

Tina: Great! Can you make it?

Edward: Yes, it would be my pleasure!

Tina: I look forward to seeing you! Oh, don't forget to <u>RSVP</u> and bring anyone you like.

Edward：我收到派對邀請函了。
Tina：太好了！你會來嗎？
Edward：會。我的榮幸！
Tina：真期待看到你！對了，歡迎攜伴參加，也別忘了回覆出席與否喔！

邀請函（invitations）英語小常識

- RSVP（répondez s'il vous plait）：RSVP（請回覆出席與否）這個法語用法在英語世界已非常普及，小心！千萬別寫成這個常見的錯誤句：「Please RSVP.」，因為RSVP中已經包含法語的「請」。

- BYOB（bring your own beverages）：（可）自備飲料。

- TBD（to be discussed）：有待討論。

- pregame（a get together before the actual party）：派對正式開始前，大家陸續聚在一起的（非正式）活動，通常是打招呼聊天、認識新朋友、先用飲料或開胃菜、小點，等待正式聚會開始。

A Guide to the Broadway Shows
百老匯看戲教戰手冊！

紐約時代廣場一向是百老匯迷們朝聖看戲的據點之一。到不了紐約沒關係，百老匯也是有遠渡重洋到訪台灣的時候！本篇文章帶讀者學習百老匯相關英語用語，並附上購票情境對話，讓你下回在看戲前，更有概念。

Broadway theatre has been widely considered to represent the highest level of commercial theatre in the English-speaking world.

在英語世界裡，百老匯劇院一直被視為商業劇場的最高呈現。

到底什麼是百老匯？看看以下這段英語：

Broadway is a theatrical performance presented in one of the 40 professional theatres (with 500 or more seats) located in the Theatre District centered along Broadway, and in Lincoln Center, in Manhattan in New York City, along with London's West End Theatre.

「百老匯」指的是以下劇場的表演：紐約百老匯街上聚集40間戲院的劇院區（每間至少配備500個座位）、林肯中心和紐約市曼哈頓的劇院、還有倫敦的西街劇院。

而劇院依據票房賣座和受歡迎的程度，又按地理位置分為百老匯音樂劇（Broadway）、外百老匯戲劇（Off Broadway）、外外百老匯戲劇（Off Off Broadway），從曼哈頓時代廣場的劇院區往外街分布。

（模擬百老匯劇院門口購票處的張貼資訊）

 Monday thru Sunday Evenings:
   Selected Orchestra & Front Mezzanine rows $97

 Saturday & Sunday Matinees
   (, including Friday Matinee on 11/23):
   Selected Orchestra & Front Mezzanine $92

 Rear Mezzanine rows $69.50: All performances

 每週一至週日晚：
   部分包廂區和第一區前排座位，票價美金97元。

 每週六和週日午後（包括11/23週五午後）：
   部分包廂區和前排座位，票價美金92元。

 每場演出的第一區後排座位，票價美金69.50元。

Broadway goers: Hi, how are you? I'd like to go to the Sunday show. Any tickets available?

Theatre box office: Yes, we provide tickets ranged from $69.50 to $97 on Sundays. Where would you like to have your row?

Broadway goers: Would it be the partial view in the rear mezzanine rows?

Theatre box office: I'm afraid so.

Broadway goers: Oh well, I think I'll buy front mezzanine to fully enjoy the show.

看戲觀眾：你好，我想看週日的表演，還有票嗎？

售票櫃檯：有的。週日的票價從美金69.50元到美金97元不等。你希望坐在哪排？

看戲觀眾：第一區的後排會不會視線被擋到？

售票櫃檯：恐怕會喔。

看戲觀眾：這樣啊。那我還是買第一區的前排，好好享受這場表演。

劇院英語小知識

· 劇院術語中，票價最高的兩區分別是Orchestra（包廂區）、Mezzanine（一樓第一區）。

· 白天午後的表演，在劇場中不用英語afternoon（中午），而是用法語matinee（中午）。

· 紐約客一般都稱曼哈頓劇院區的購票櫃檯為theatre office box，不是counter。而因為英語「去劇院」的講法「go to (the theatre)」動詞使用go，看戲的觀眾便被叫做goers。以此類推，電影觀眾就是movie goers。

Travel Agent <u>Evolution</u>

旅遊業再進化：新型態旅遊相關英語

越來越多消費者懂得善用網路資源，不需透過旅行社便可自行規劃行程並訂房訂票，因此傳統旅遊業者不得不轉型。本文帶讀者用英語觀點一窺旅遊業的進化，並了解幾種旅遊型態。

With the boom of Internet booking sites, the traditional travel agent is an endangered species! CareerCast recently included travel agents in its roundup of "useless jobs."

傳統旅遊業者小心了！隨著網路上自助訂票系統的發達，你們已經是瀕臨絕種的物種了！甚至連美國求職網站CareerCast，近期都已將旅遊業仲介綜述為「無用的職位」。

But then the travel agents had this <u>revolution</u>, and below are some areas and categories where travel agents are still succeeding:

不過旅遊業者也有了革命轉型，以下列出幾種領域和旅遊型態，消費者仍會找上旅遊仲介：

- **corporate travel 員工旅遊（口語英語也可用company trip）**

When it comes to business travel, most people don't check online. They just want to book.

若今天旅遊型態是公司舉辦的員工旅遊，大部分的人並不會自行上網搜尋比價，只想直接下訂。

- **luxury 奢華行程**

It is reported that the luxury travelers tend to talk to someone with experiences, and this is why the luxury market works well under the travel agency model.

據報導，負擔得起奢華旅遊的消費者，傾向於委託有經驗的旅遊專員，這也讓旅遊業者得以承辦這些頂級行程，而繼續以仲介型態經營其商業模式。

- **cruises 遊輪行程**

For cruise travels, agents still book these more often than the individuals.

就遊輪旅遊而言，旅遊業者所下訂的行程還是比自助旅行的散戶多。

- **complicated and important trips 特別重要的個別行程**

For very important trips, such as once-in-a-lifetime honeymoon, people tend to ask travel agents to customize their trips.

這種旅遊行程通常是一生一次的蜜月（honeymoon），因此會透過旅遊業者量身訂做。

- **emerging markets 新興市場**

In Mainland China, where large numbers of the first-time travelers are heading overseas, it's common to travel with an organized tour.

在中國大陸，許多第一次出國旅遊的民眾，普遍透過旅行社的規劃參加團體旅遊。

焦點英語

- **evolution [ˌɛvə'luʃən] (n.)** 進化、演化

  e.g. The scientists have been studying the origins and the evolution of modern cetaceans.

  例句 科學家一直以來都在研究近代鯨豚的起源和演化。

- **revolution [ˌrɛvə'luʃən] (n.)** 革命

  e.g. The industrialization first brought the world the revolution of transportation to the world before the modern manufacturing.

  例句 工業化首先帶給世界交通運輸上的革命，再來就是近代製造業。

The New Travel Guide to the Fiesta (1): Festivals around the World

旅遊新指南（上）：英語世界慶典

語言學習裡，參與文化活動非常有益。本文列出幾個英語系國家的嘉年華、音樂季和慶典，讓你在計畫下回的旅遊前，對英語世界有更深度的探索與文化認識！

Ever felt that you didn't get to see the best part of a city on your trip? Are you looking to join some of the world's best celebrations and cultural showcases? There's a list of events by month, showing you some famous festivals held in the English speaking countries.

曾經覺得過往旅行沒有機會見識到當地城市特色嗎？有興趣出席世界著名的慶典和文化盛事嗎？以下按月份列出幾個英語國家的嘉年華、藝術節、音樂祭。

Month 月份	Festivals 慶典活動
January 一月	· Winter Carnival, Quebec, Canada 加拿大魁北克，冬季嘉年華
February 二月	· White Night Melbourne, Melbourne, Australia 澳洲墨爾本，白夜通宵嘉年華 · New Orleans Mardi Gras, USA 美國紐奧良，馬蒂·格拉斯狂歡嘉年華（與巴西、威尼斯嘉年華並列世界三大嘉年華）
March 三月	· Hong Kong Arts Festival, Hong Kong 香港，香港藝術節 · St. Patrick's Festival, Dublin, Ireland 愛爾蘭都柏林，聖派翠克節 · Moisture Festival (Comedy and Theatre), Seattle, USA 美國西雅圖，劇場藝術滑水節
April 四月	· Speyside Whisky Festival, Scotland, UK 蘇格蘭，酒鄉斯佩賽威士忌酒節 · Melbourne International Comedy Festival, Melbourne, Australia 澳洲墨爾本，墨爾本國際喜劇藝術節
May 五月	· Vienna Festival, Austria 奧地利，維也納藝術節
June 六月	· Glastonbury Music Festival, UK 英國，格拉斯頓伯里音樂祭（目前全世界最大的露天搖滾音樂祭）

Month 月份	Festivals 慶典活動
July 七月	· Toronto Fringe Festival (Theatre), Canada 加拿大，多倫多表演藝術藝穗節 · Rainforest World Music Festival, Borneo, Malaysia 馬來西亞婆羅洲，世界雨林音樂祭
August 八月	· Notting Hill Carnival, London, UK 英國倫敦，諾丁丘嘉年華 · International Balloon Fiesta, Bristol, UK 英國布里斯托，國際熱氣球節 · Vancouver International Jazz Festival, Canada 加拿大，溫哥華國際爵士樂嘉年華 · Burning Man, Black Rock City, NV, USA 美國內華達州，黑石沙漠，燃燒人慶典，又名火人祭
September 九月	· New York Musical Theatre Festival, USA 美國，紐約音樂劇劇場藝術節 · San Francisco Blues Festival, USA 美國舊金山，藍調音樂嘉年華
October 十月	· Canterbury Arts Festival, England, UK 英格蘭，侃特伯里藝術節
November 十一月	· Macy's Thanksgiving Day Parade, New York City, USA 美國紐約，梅西百貨感恩節大遊行
December 十二月	· New Year's Eve, Sydney, Australia 澳洲雪梨，新年跨年 · New Year's Eve, Times Square, New York City, USA 美國紐約，時代廣場新年跨年

The New Travel Guide to the Fiesta (2): Festival Survival Guide

旅遊新指南（下）：慶典、嘉年華教戰手冊

上篇介紹了幾個英語系國家的嘉年華和慶典，這回帶讀者以英語觀點來注意參加時該小心的事項，期盼讀者都能有機會來場英語深度旅遊。

Festival goers and tourists, if you plan to go to the music festivals overseas, there are more than 300 summer music festivals in the UK and Ireland. Some of the famous and the biggest festivals involve camping. How to get fully prepared enjoy the festivals? Read the <u>survival</u> tips below suggested by experienced travelers around the world.

如果你剛好是熱愛參加戶外音樂祭、嘉年華的人，或是想有海外深度旅遊的觀光，光是英國和愛爾蘭在夏天就有超過300場戶外音樂祭。其中幾個最有名的大型音樂祭通常都需要民眾露營參加。如何充分準備並好好享受？請看以下綜合各路旅人經驗老到的分享。

- **Settle in earlier.**
  早早卡位。

Arrive early and pitch your tent within sight of landmarks that you'll remember even when you wake up to a field covered by thousands of tents. In addition, choose a spot far away from the toilets because it won't be long before they stink.

早點抵達現場,最好把你的帳篷設在視線可及有明顯地標處,以免一覺醒來只看到上千座帳篷在同一個場地。此外,紮營處離廁所遠一點,免得沒多久後就開始有異味。

- **Leave it home.**
  能不帶出門的就留在家吧。

Keep valuables, like money, IDs or passport with you. Don't bring more than you need. Never leave things you can't afford to lose in your tent.

貴重物品請隨身攜帶,例如現金、身分證、護照。不需要的就別帶去現場,也別把你丟不得的貴重物品留在帳篷裡。

- **Carry a cheap camera.**
  用便宜的相機就好。

Do you really want to carry a heavy, digital SLR (single lens reflex) around your neck for the whole festival? Instead, invest a cheaper pocket digital camera or disposable film camera. Or, you can just rely on your smart phone with camera in it.

整個音樂祭全程，你不會想在脖子上一直掛著沉甸甸的單眼相機。反而投資便宜點的小台數位相機比較實際，或是拋棄式的底片相機。不然，就依賴智慧型手機的相機。

- **Just say no.**
  向毒品說不。

Drugs will probably be everywhere, and so will the cops.

毒品可能到時隨處可見，警察也是。

- **Watch your drinking.**
  注意飲酒。

Be careful with what you drink and who you accept drinks from. Take it slow. You don't want to end up waking up outside your tent.

小心你喝的杯中物和給你飲料的人。慢慢喝，你可不想最後在你帳篷外的地方醒來。

- **Last but not the least; stay safe with a group.**
  最後，但也是很重要的一點，跟著人群、注意安全。

Always keep in touch with your friends and tell your friends where and when you expect to meet up.

隨時和朋友保持聯繫，並告訴友人你們預期何時在哪邊會合。

· **survival [sə'vaɪv!] (n.) / survive [sə'vaɪv] (v.)**

生還、存活、全身而退

e.g. Some of the residents managed to <u>survive</u> the massive earth-quake and returned home to clean up the mess two days after.

例句 一部分的居民想辦法從這場強震存活下來，並在2天後重返家園清理殘局。

10 Cities Where Bicycles Rule the Streets (1)

世界10大自行車城市（上）

台北市等有微笑單車YouBike在各大捷運站外供民眾租借，其他各大城市也早有便民的公共自行車租借系統。來看看世界10大自行車城市，了解其他城市的租借單車名稱和生活文化風情。

進入本文前，請先想想以下詞彙的英語怎麼說：

A. 公共自行車（租借）系統

B. 交通堵塞

C. 單車愛好者

答案就在本文中！

- **Paris zooms ahead**
  巴黎，全球第一大自行車之都

Parisians have been able to rent Velib bikes since July 2007. The city has over 20,000 bikes at 1800 stations. It is the biggest **(A)bike sharing system** in the world, sponsored by the Paris Town Hall and France's outdoor advertising group JC Decaux. Experts say private-public partnerships are the best model for bike sharing success.

巴黎市民早在2007年便開始享受自行車租借，整個城市的公共自行車系統「Velib」已經遍及1,800個租借站，擁有超過20,000台自行車。巴黎的

Velib自行車由巴黎市政廳和歐洲最大的戶外廣告商德高集團所贊助。專家指出，這種公立私營合作的方式，是公共自行車系統成功經營的最佳典範。

- **New York gets Citi Bike**
  紐約，企業贊助單車

New York launched its Citi Bike sharing system on Memorial Day for members (public use will follow). About 330 stations in Manhattan and Brooklyn will have thousands of bicycles for rent. Citi Bike has been <u>in the works</u> since 2011, and Citibank signed up as the primary corporate sponsor.

紐約市在美國國殤日（5月的最後一個星期一）發起公共自行車租借系統「Citi」，先只開放給會員使用，接著會普及大眾。預計在曼哈頓和布魯克林區將設立330個自行車站，上千台自行車供民眾租借。紐約的Citi Bike自2011年開始籌建，而花旗銀行（Citi Bank）就是主要贊助商。

- **London and its Boris Bikes**
  倫敦，市民親暱的自行車租借

London Santander Cycles bicycles <u>went into operation</u> in 2010. The program, nicknamed Boris Bikes because of the city's bike riding mayor, marked an effort to cut down on **(B)traffic congestion** and lead the sprawling city to a cleaner, greener future. London has 10,000 bikes at 700 stations, including the British Museum and Buckingham Palace. Prince William is also among the city's regular **(C) cycling enthusiasts**.

倫敦的自行車租借「Santander Cycles」在2010年開始營運，被倫敦市民暱稱為「Boris Bikes」。其暱稱來自身體力行騎自行車的倫敦市長（Boris

Johnson），他致力於推行自行車通勤，大幅改善了交通壅塞，力求還給市民一個更乾淨、更綠化的未來。倫敦目前有700個自行車租借站，10,000台自行車營運中。租借站包括了大英博物館和白金漢宮。威廉王子也是倫敦自行車愛好者之一。

- ### Montreal expands its Bixi program
  ### 蒙特婁，公共自行車系統全面擴大中

Although Montreal can be covered in snow weeks longer than other North American cities, it has become a Mecca for bike sharing enthusiasts. The Bixi program added new stations this past year, bringing its total to 460 stations with 5,200 bikes. Bixi began in 2009. Its name is a combination of "bicycle" and "taxi."

位於北美洲的蒙特婁，無畏其每年的寒冬有好幾週被白雪覆蓋，仍是自行車愛好者的朝聖之地，且市政府依舊持續擴展市區自行車租借站的普及度。蒙特婁的單車系統「Bixi」，在去年剛增設了更多租借站，總數擴增到460個租借站，5,200台自行車。Bixi始於2009年，名字發想於自行車（bicycle）和計程車（taxi）的英文字組合。

- ### Amsterdam, a bike crazy city
  ### 阿姆斯特丹，全民瘋單車

There are more bicycles than people in Amsterdam, the world's most enthusiastic bike riding city. Bicyclists pushed to keep a special passageway open at the Rijksmuseum, which reopened in May 2015 after a 10-year renovation. Architects and <u>successive</u> museum directors had opposed allowing bikes through, and a local government tried to have them barred on safety grounds. But the cyclists stood their ground.

在阿姆斯特丹，單車的數量遠比人口多！市民熱愛單車的程度讓這裡成為名副其實的自行車之都。歷時10年的整修後，2015年5月重新開館的阿姆斯特丹國家博物館，甚至開了一條單車道給騎士們通過。建築家和連續幾任博物館館長原本都反對博物館單車道的點子，連當地政府都曾試著要騎士們繞道。不過最後的結果讓大家看到這座城市有多瘋自行車。

焦點英語

· **in the works**　計畫中、籌建、擬定中

e.g. A plan of reorganization is reported to be now <u>in the works</u>.

例句 據報導，一項改組計畫正在擬定中。

· **go into operation**　開始營運、生效、運轉、運作

e.g. The factory machines finally <u>went into operation</u>.

例句 工廠機器終於開始運轉。

· **successive [sək'sɛsɪv] (adj.)**　連續的、接連……

e.g. This school team has won three <u>successive</u> games.

　　= This school team has won three games <u>in a row</u>.

例句 這隻校隊已連勝3場比賽。（口語英語中的in a row也可表達「連續」）

10 Cities Where Bicycles Rule the Streets (2)

世界10大自行車城市（下）

節能減碳不只是全球趨勢，更是愛地球的實際行動。自行車絕對是交通上更愛地球的選擇。上篇介紹了巴黎、紐約、倫敦、蒙特婁、阿姆斯特丹的自行車現象，繼續來看看下篇的5個自行車城市。

進入本文前，請先想想以下詞彙的英語怎麼說：

A. 市郊

B. 單車道

C. 提倡、鼓吹

答案就在本文中！

• Boston, the Hub and its Hubway
波士頓，公共自行車四通八達至市郊

For years, many people have gotten away without owning cars in Boston, preferring to walk or take the T. Now, some are hopping on bikes. The Hubway, Boston's bike sharing system, has 140 stations and 1,300 bikes. It sells annual and monthly memberships, along with hourly rentals. And its stations are popping up in the **(A)suburbs**, too.

波士頓居民多年來捨棄開車，偏好他們暱稱為「T」的地鐵，或甚至步行，有些則開始靠單車通勤，因此而發展出公共自行車系統「Hubway」。目前整個

系統有140個自行車租借站，1,300輛自行車供民眾租借，分為一年制會員、月票、還有以小時計算的租借方式。自行車租借站甚至從市中心遍及市郊。

• Chattanooga, Tenneesse: Chattanoogans cruise along the city streets
田納西州，查塔努加，市民單車遨遊街頭

Visitors to Chattanooga are sometimes surprised to discover the Bicycle Transit System, which puts the southern city in the same league as bigger, better known capitols. The city has 300 bicycles at 33 stations, and members can ride for an hour <u>at a time</u> as part of their annual membership.

到查塔努加，遊客會驚訝於當地的公共自行車系統，便利的程度讓這個南方小城市的名氣不亞於首都。整個城市有33個自行車租借站和300台自行車。租借自行車還有會員制，只要成為一年份的付費會員，便可以獲得一小時內旅程免費（不限次數）的福利。

• Students ride through Stanford
史丹佛，大學生單車穿梭校園

The first thing visitors to Stanford University notice is the steady stream of bicycles, gliding around the campus. Stanford, with 20,000 students, and an <u>estimated</u> 15,000 bikes, is a platinum level bicycle friendly university, with its own Campus Bicycle Coordinator.

初到史丹佛大學城，一定會注意到不斷穿梭往來校園間的自行車。史丹佛的20,000名學生有15,000台自行車，在學校組織對自行車的管理推行下，成為大學生普遍騎乘自行車的友善大學城。

- **San Francisco on wheels**
  舊金山，隨處可見單車道

Everywhere you look in San Francisco, you'll find bikes to rent. With 12,000 members, the San Francisco Bicycle Coalition is the largest bicycle advocacy organization in the country. Through its efforts, the city has doubled the number of **(B)bike paths**, and **(C)advocates** are pushing for a connected bicycle network across San Francisco.

在舊金山，你會發現到處都能租借單車。目前的自行車租借系統共有12,000個會員，為全美最大的自行車租借城市。也因為一直以來提倡自行車，舊金山的單車道更是倍數增加中，甚至有聲浪促使連結各個單車道，更加便民。

- **Portland, land of bicycles**
  波特蘭，自行車之鄉

Portland, Oregon, may not be Paris or Amsterdam, but it has plenty of bicycle enthusiasts. There are bikes for rent, bikes for sale and an abundance of bicycle tours. Even police in Portland ride bicycles when they have to <u>deal with</u> protestors.

雖然不能和巴黎或阿姆斯特丹相比，波特蘭也是有廣大的單車愛好者。除了自行車租借系統外，還有自行車販賣，以及豐富的自行車觀光行程。就連波特蘭的警察在面對抗議群眾時，也是騎自行車待命的。

焦點英語

· **at a time**　每次、在某時

e.g. If only problems would come one <u>at a time</u>!

例句 要是一次只發生一個問題就好了！

· **estimated ['ɛstəˌmetɪd] (adj.)**　預估的、估計的

e.g. It is <u>estimated</u> that the rain will last for four days.

例句 估計這次會下個4天的雨。

· **deal with**　處理、應付

e.g. She <u>deals with</u> customers on the phone and rarely meet them face-to-face.

例句 她大部分在電話上處理客戶的問題，很少和他們面對面接觸。

Chapter 3

Food and Beverages

餐飲英語

A Sweet Tooth:
Can't Resist the Taste of Dessert?

什麼是「甜牙齒」？學習甜點英語用語

無法抗拒甜食的誘惑嗎？飯後習慣來上一份甜點，為那頓餐食畫下完美的句點嗎？來學習甜點相關的英語用語，搭配有趣的例句和情境對話，讓你不只敢開口品嚐，更敢開口說英語！

下面兩句英語，真正的中文意思是什麼？

1. I was born with a <u>sweet tooth</u>, and the cavities are the proofs to it!

英語字面上的翻譯：「我生來就有甜牙齒，這些蛀牙就是證明！」

什麼是「甜牙齒」？和蛀牙（單數名詞cavity）又有什麼關係？原來這句英語是出自一位愛吃甜食者的口中，而英語就用「with a sweet tooth」或「have a sweet tooth」，來形容如筆者一樣嗜甜如命的甜食愛好者。

所以，以中文的邏輯來翻譯，這是一句俏皮話：「我超愛吃甜食，看看我這些蛀牙就知道了！」例句中的「I was born with a sweet tooth.」也可以直接說成「I have a sweet tooth.」。

2. My sister makes <u>killer desserts</u>. Her cheesecake is something to die for!

英語字面上的翻譯：「我姊做的是殺手級甜點。她的起士蛋糕讓人死也甘願！」

這句英語用的killer和to die for都是誇飾法，是對於料理極大的恭維！「killer desserts」表示「這甜點堪稱一絕、無人相匹敵」。

所以，以中文的邏輯來翻譯，就是：「我姊做的甜點堪稱一絕，好吃死了！」而例句中的「Her cheesecake is something to die for!」也可以說成「Her cheesecake is divine!」。

情境對話

(at the dining table after dinner)

Debbie: How is the brownie?

Samuel: It's out of this world! Even my wife likes it, and she's a picky eater!

Debbie: Please give me a piece of that. I'll try it.

（晚餐後的餐桌上）
Debbie：這個布朗尼味道如何？
Samuel：好吃到不行啊！
連我太太都愛，她對吃可是很挑的喔！
Debbie：讓我嚐一塊看看。

・Sundae? Sunday? 「聖代」的英語由來：

According to Oxford English Dictionary, the spelling and pronunciation of "sundae" derive from "Sunday". And it has been generally accepted with the origin of the Sunday laws, a.k.a. the Blue Laws, in 1890 in Illinois in the United States, where they outlawed the sale of ice cream on Sundays. Hence, the invention of sundae came with scoops of ice cream topped with fruits, whipped cream and nuts with the sauce of syrup.

這道和Sunday發音一樣且拼字相似的冰淇淋甜點，英語出處的確源自Sunday一字！根據牛津英語字典，美國伊利諾州在1890年曾頒佈「週日冰淇淋消費禁令」。遂有人發明了加上水果、糖漿、堅果、鮮奶油等配料的甜點，因在週日販賣，便取名Sundae（聖代），既不違反法律、又能吃到以冰淇淋為主體的甜點！

Poor Boy?

這是潛艇堡？口語英語好有趣！

口語英語該怎麼用？隱含著什麼文化歷史背景？本文介紹兩個英語詞彙，帶你從文化面來學道地美式英語。

先來閱讀下面兩段英語對話，到底裡面的boy分別是什麼意思？跟「男孩」有沒有關係？

1. "poor boy?"

Christopher: I'm gonna make <u>poor boys</u> for the picnic in the park this coming weekend.

Emma: Yum! I'll bring some lemonade over. See you in the park then!

Christopher：我要做些潛艇堡帶去這週末的公園野餐。

Emma：好吃耶！我會帶一些檸檬水過去。到時公園裡見！

2. "oh boy?"

Emma: I'm so happy that the rainy season's finally over.

Christopher: Yeah but it's the typhoon season now.

Emma: <u>Oh boy</u>!

Emma：好開心，梅雨季終於結束了。
Christopher：對呀，但現在是颱風季節了。
Emma：天啊！

對話2裡，Emma的回應是感嘆詞，這時的oh boy等同於oh my god或oh really的驚訝口氣。

原來同樣一個英語字，在不同的對話情境裡有完全不一樣的意思。

對話1裡的「poor boy」是美式英語潛艇堡的一種名稱，完全不能直接照字面上翻譯成「窮小子」或「可憐人」！不然就鬧笑話了。這說法起源於美國南部路易西安那州（Louisiana）紐奧良（New Orleans），又可說「po boy」。

1920年代末期經濟大蕭條（The Recession），許多人因此失業，當時有好心人在路邊免費供應這種在法國長麵包（baguette）裡包肉或海鮮的三明治，餵飽很多人。

這時代背景有一插曲為，每次只要有免費供應的潛艇堡，就會有人指著來拿取潛艇堡的人說：「See! Here comes the poor boy!」（看！可憐人來〔拿潛艇堡〕了！）。因此沿用至今，poor boy成為長型三明治的英語說法，也成為紐奧良的代表菜之一。

The Cubicle Cuisine VS.
The Healthy Lifestyle Choices

辦公室用餐 VS. 健康新選擇

> 上班族們，你怎麼渡過午休時間呢？叫外賣到辦公室？約見客戶或應酬？外出用餐順便透氣？在辦公桌前享用自己準備的便當？還是一邊用餐一邊趕工？本文搭配情境會話，帶讀者認識辦公室用餐的相關英語用語。

「辦公室用餐」、「午休」、「帶便當」的英語怎麼說？

Cubicle cuisine can be a sign of multitasking sometimes. Office people take a lunch break, some; however, use it to work while having their meals delivered to the desks.

在辦公室裡用餐，這有時候是工作量到了極致的結果。上班族們有午休時間，然而有些人卻得利用午餐時間一邊工作，直接叫外送到辦公室裡。

Many people do the meal prep at home and pack their lunch to the office as a healthier and more economic food choice.

許多人自己在家準備好食物，帶便當到辦公室，也不失為一種更健康經濟的選擇。

中文裡的「帶便當」，英語文化裡說的是「準備食物、餐食」：food preparation / meal preparation，最常聽到的說法為口語英語：meal prep（preparation的縮寫）。

Laura: Hi, Michael. Where were you yesterday?

Michael: Hi Laura! I went to the doctor.

Laura: Oh really? What's wrong?

Michael: High blood pressure.

Laura: That's dangerous! What did the doctor say?

Michael: The doctor said no more fast food and cubicle cuisine at the office.

Laura: I see. You can start your meal prep for the lunch. Nothing's better than your own food.

Michael: Oh the doctor also said it's not just the food. It's being stuck at my office desk all day and not moving around enough.

Laura: Sounds like you have to leave your desk now and join us for lunch break? Let's take a walk!

Laura：嗨，Michael。你昨天去哪了？

Michael：嗨，Laura！我去看了醫生。

Laura：是喔！怎麼了？

Michael：高血壓。

Laura：那很危險耶！醫生怎麼說？

Michael：醫生說別再吃速食和在辦公室用餐了。

Laura：這樣啊。你可以開始自己準備午餐，自己做的食物最好了。

Michael：喔，醫生說不只是食物。還有我整天坐在辦公桌前，活動量不夠。

Laura：聽起來你現在就該離開辦公桌，加入我們的午休時間，

　　　　一起出去走一走吧！

· cubicle ['kjubɪkəl] (n.)　辦公室隔間

e.g. I really need to go out to get some fresh air after being stuck in the office <u>cubicle</u> all day.

例句 困在辦公室辦公隔間一整天後，我真的需要出去透透氣。

· cuisine [kwɪ'zin] (n.)　料理

許多上班族午休時間是在辦公室座位上用餐，於是衍生出了cubicle cuisine一詞。休息時間的動詞片語用法為take a break，因此「午休」的英語講法為同樣邏輯的lunch break。

e.g. The executive chef at this restaurant is famous for the authentic Italian <u>cuisine</u>.

例句 這間餐廳的行政主廚以道地義式料理聞名。

· food prep / meal prep　準備食物、食材、帶便當

prep是preparation的縮寫。

e.g. <u>Food prep</u> on Sunday nights is what I enjoy doing to get ready for another new week.

例句 我很享受每週日晚上準備食物帶便當，為接下來新的一週做好準備。

「帶便當」東西方文化大不同

　　華人世界裡，大家從小到大求學，一直到坐辦公室、出門郊遊野餐，所熟悉的「帶便當」，和英語世界有點不太一樣，西方人通常是用保鮮盒預先準備好未來一週的食物，按日期、食物種類、烹調方式來分盒。而且meal prep的主要目的更多是為了健身、營養管理、體重控制、並更有效率的在週間工作。用meal prep當英語關鍵字，查查更多網路上西方「帶便當」的畫面。

You Are What You Eat: Keep Your Meat Safe

肉品安全多重要？英語知識告訴你

台灣近幾年食品安全問題鬧得沸沸揚揚，除了食用油和牛奶的問題，肉品安全也不容小覷。本文帶讀者學習美國營養學會所提供的肉品知識，讓我們主動為吃下肚的食品把關。

"You are what you eat!" More and more people are becoming concerned about the food they eat is safe, especially when it comes to meat safety.

英語有句話說：「You are what you eat!」，意思是「你吃什麼會影響你長成什麼樣！」因此要注重飲食。越來越多人開始留意吃下肚的食物是否安全，尤其是肉品安全。

The Academy of Nutrition and Dietetics (AND), the world's largest organization of food and nutrition professionals, have been encouraging the public to take an active role in safeguarding the meat you eat.

全球最大的食物與營養組織：美國營養學會（AND）一直鼓勵大眾為吃下肚的肉品安全把關。

Read the following tips from AND to get your meat safely and eat right:

閱讀以下美國營養學會提供的肉品安全注意事項，學習如何吃得安全又正確：

· Look for the Safe Food Handling label on packages.
  This label means the meat has undergone safe processing.
  留意包裝上有無食品安全認證標籤，這代表肉品有經過安全處理。

· Make sure the meat is tightly wrapped.
  確認肉的包裝是封緊的。

· Pick your meat last when you go grocery shopping.
  購物時最後再挑選肉類。

· Eat or freeze cooked meat within three to four days.
  煮熟的肉類，3到4天內食用完畢或冷凍保存。

· Defrost meat in the refrigerator or in the microwave. Never defrost meat on the counter.
  在冰箱（下層）冷藏解凍，或用微波爐解凍肉類，千萬別在廚房流理台上解凍。

· Do not re-freeze thawed meat.
  勿重複冷凍已退冰解凍的肉類。

· Marinate meat in the refrigerator.
  醃肉時，放在冰箱裡。

· Do not leave cooked meat out of refrigerator for more than two hours.
  煮熟的肉類不要離開冰箱超過2小時。

· Use two separate cutting boards: One for raw meat and another for fruits and vegetable. This helps prevent cross-contamination.
  使用兩個獨立的砧板：一個切生肉，另一個切蔬果。這可預防交叉感染。

Julia: I'm having a BBQ on Saturday.

Will you have some free time to join us?

Sam: Sounds great! I'm in.

And I'd love to go grocery shopping with you.

Julia: Awesome!

I'll need your help at the butcher shop to pick some beef.

Sam: No problem. I can do that with the tips from the AND.

Julia：我週六要烤肉，你有空一起來嗎？

Sam：聽起來很棒耶！算我一份！我也很樂意和妳一起去採買食物喔。

Julia：太好了！到時需要你幫我一起在肉鋪挑些牛肉。

Sam：沒問題。就照著美國營養學會提供的訣竅。

焦點英語

· **thaw [θɔ] (v.)**　解凍、融雪、透過逐漸升溫的融化、變得暖活、緩和

e.g. In the mountains here, it doesn't <u>thaw</u> in the summer.

例句 這裡的山區夏天也不會融雪。

· **contamination [ɪn'fɛkʃən] (n.)**　感染、傳染

e.g. It is extremely important to prevent <u>contamination</u> in the lab.

例句 在實驗室裡，預防感染極為重要。

Breakfast or Brunch?
Get Your Meals Right

早餐還是早午餐？英語這樣點

> 歐美世界的早午餐，在台灣已經流行多年，甚至全日早午餐（all-day brunch）也到處都吃得到。本文帶讀者從英語對話中學習英語點餐的方式，並學習西式早餐中，雞蛋的幾種烹調選擇，讓你點餐更有變化。

到底什麼是brunch？

這個可愛的英語字，是早餐（breakfast）和午餐（lunch）的組合。特別盛行於週末放假時，是大家可以不用那麼早起的餐飲選擇。

情境對話

Customer: Excuse me, I know it's now 4 p.m., but do you still serve brunch?

Server: Yes, we have all-day brunch at this restaurant. Here is the menu.

Customer: Great. Thank you. I think I'll have the American breakfast.

Server: How would you like your eggs done?

Customer: Scrambled, please. And please make sure they aren't too runny.

Server: Sure. And would you like bacon, ham or sausages?

Customer: Bacon sounds good. Make it crispy, please.

Server: We also serve rye bread and whole wheat bread. Which do you prefer?

Customer: I'll have the whole-wheat. Thanks.

客人：不好意思，我知道現在是下午4點，不過還有供應早午餐嗎？

服務生：有的，我們餐廳有供應全日早午餐，菜單在這裡。

客人：太好了，謝謝你。我想，我點美式早餐好了。

服務生：請問您的蛋要如何製作？

客人：炒蛋，謝謝，請幫我確認不要太生。

服務生：好的。那請問您要培根、火腿、還是香腸？

客人：培根聽起來不錯，請幫我做脆一點。

服務生：我們還會附黑麥麵包或全麥麵包，請問您偏好哪一種？

客人：我要全麥的，謝謝。

餐飲英語雞蛋小常識

　　西式早餐和早午餐中附的雞蛋，有多種烹調方式可以選擇，除了上述對話中的炒蛋（scrambled），另外還有以下幾種受歡迎的吃法：

· fried eggs 煎蛋
　另外還有sunny-side up（蛋黃未熟的太陽蛋）的吃法。

· omelets 蛋捲

· poached eggs 水波蛋

· eggs Benedict 班尼迪克蛋
　將兩顆去殼且半熟的poached eggs（水波蛋）置於English muffins
　（英式鬆糕）上的吃法。

　　下回在英語世界點餐，試試看其他吃法吧！

Winter Comfort Foods in Taiwan

就是這一味！台灣的暖冬療癒食物

台灣的冬天有很多有名的美食，大部份為鍋物料理（hot pot），或是養生湯品（soup），且幾乎都有冬季進補的養生功效（medical effect）。部份餐廳甚至生意好到僅在冬季營業，這對於外國人來說，是個不可思議的現象。本文帶讀者用英語認識台灣特有的冬季珍饈。

薑母鴨、麻油雞、羊肉爐、藥燉排骨，這些台灣冬季美食的英語，你知道該怎麼說嗎？又該如何向外國人介紹呢？

吃了滿足、讓人感到「療癒」的食物，英語是這樣形容的：comfort food。

來看看以下受歡迎的台灣冬季comfort foods英語怎麼說：

‧ginger duck hot pot 薑母鴨

Ginger duck hot pot in Taiwan is so popular in the winter that the restaurants serving it only need to open for three to four months in the winter. The dish is served hot pot style and the real flavor of the soup comes from the stock, based in pure rice wine, Chinese herbs, dried fruits such as red dates, Goji berries and Chinese angelica roots. Diners add more meat and raw vegetables while it's served.

薑母鴨在台灣冬季受歡迎到什麼程度呢？薑母鴨餐廳只需在冬天營業3到4個月。這道鍋物主要的風味來自其高湯：純米酒、中藥材、紅棗、枸杞、當歸。上桌後，用餐者再往鍋裡添加更多鴨肉和生鮮蔬菜。

- **chicken soup in sesame oil 麻油雞**

It is made with generous amounts of sesame oil, ginger slices and Taiwanese rice wine. This Taiwanese chicken soup is long believed to stimulate <u>blood circulation</u>, boost the <u>immune system</u> and speed up the <u>metabolism</u>. Also, this is often served to new mothers after giving birth.

由大量的麻油、薑片、米酒煮成。這道台式雞湯長久以來被認為可促進血液循環、增強免疫系統、加速新陳代謝。還有，這也是生產後的婦女常飲用的湯品。

- **lamb stewed in Chinese herbs 羊肉爐**

This dark-colored broth, often cooked in a clay pot, works wonder for driving away winter shivers on a cold night. According to the 16th-century "Compendium of Materia Medica," a comprehensive text on traditional Chinese herbal medicine, lamb meat is excellent to help restore energy, generate inner body heat and even strengthen kidneys.

這道深色高湯料理通常放在陶鍋燉煮，對於冬夜裡的畏寒特有奇效。根據16世紀的本草綱目記載，羊肉最棒的是可幫助恢復體力、暖身子，並強化腎臟功能。

- **pork rib soup in Chinese herbs 藥膳排骨／藥燉排骨**

Taiwanese cuisine is famous for its soupy dishes with the medical effects, and this pork rib soup is definitely one of the must-have delicacies. The pork rib in this winter soup is so tender that it falls right off the bone when it's served. Chinese herbal specialists often recommend this to those with the chronic cold hands and feet.

台式料理有名在於有很多的養生藥膳湯品，藥膳排骨絕對是非吃不可的一道。上桌後的排骨在湯裡就可立刻和骨頭分離，入口即化。中藥專家更是經常推薦給季節性手腳冰冷者食用。

· **blood circulation [blʌd ˌsɝkjə'leʃən]** 血液循環

e.g. The <u>blood circulation</u> in your body plays an important role in your overall health.

例句 身體中的血液循環在整體健康上扮演了重要的角色。

· **immune system [ɪ'mjoon 'sɪstəm]** 免疫系統

e.g. Are you doing all you can do to strengthen your <u>immune system</u>?

例句 你有盡你所能去加強免疫系統嗎？

· **metabolism [mɪ'tæbəˌlɪzəm] (n.)** 新陳代謝

e.g. Your body gets the energy it needs through a process called <u>metabolism</u>.

例句 你身體所需的能量是透過新陳代謝這個過程來獲得。

英語美食小常識

　　看完這些冬季美食，是不是胃口大開，想吃得不得了？英語用crave這個動詞表達想吃某樣美食的心情。

e.g. I've been <u>craving</u> ginger duck hot pot, and it's now finally the winter where there are soupy places everywhere in Taiwan. I'm in heaven!

例句 我一直都好想吃薑母鴨喔，冬天終於被我等到了，台灣到處都有熱湯的料理，我簡直是在美食天堂！

otorcar in the early 20th century. Railway companies in Europe and the United States used streamlined tra
33 for high-speed services with an average speed of up to 130 km/h (80 mph) and a top speed of more than 1
0 mph). The first high-speed train was the Italian ETR 200 that in July 1939 went from Milan to Florence at
th a top speed of 203 km/h. With this service, these trains were able to compete with the upcoming airplan
the Odakyu Electric Railway in Greater Tokyo launched its Romancecar 3000 SSE. This set a world record
auge trains at 145 km/h (90 mph), giving Japanese designers confidence that they could safely build even fas

Chapter 4

At the Office
辦公室現象

Are You the Stepford Worker?

你在老闆眼中是哪種員工？

職場上、辦公室生態（office politics）裡，雇主（employer）把什麼人才放在什麼位置，真是再重要不過了！本文要來介紹兩種類型員工（employee）的英語講法。

• Stepford Worker
盲目效忠、毫無想法的員工

Stepford一詞來自於小說《*The Stepford Wives*》，也有被製作成同名電影，台灣譯為《超完美嬌妻》，由妮可基嫚（Nicole Kidman）主演。故事描述在紐約市郊區的一個虛構小鎮裡，有一群完美的賢妻良母，事實上卻是肉身的機器人，毫無個人思想，並順服於丈夫。

職場（corporative world）上，Stepford Worker是指那些「盲目效忠於公司、主管、政策，賣命工作，但卻毫無想法的員工（an employee who follows the company line so closely as to become an unthinking clone）」。

辦公室情境例句：

I'm afraid we have to let someone go. However, we're between the devil and the deep blue sea. Jack's a compliant Stepford Worker, who'd go along like a good old Stepford. Derek's energetic, spunky and original, but he has a mind of his own.

恐怕我們必須裁掉一名員工，但兩者真的很難抉擇。Jack是個順從的超完美員工，總是附和公司的決定和政策。Derek精力充沛、趕做敢為又有原創性，但太有主見。

• Clocksucker
沒有顯著工作表現的員工

這種員工就真的讓老闆頭痛了！這類型的員工，當初應徵時會被雇用，可能是仗著有點小聰明，但又不是絕頂聰明。從老闆和主管眼中看來，clocksucker任職後，「是一個沒有顯著工作表現的員工，耗了許久也只能完成一件小事，好像在浪費老闆的錢（a clever, but not terribly subtle employee who does no work and wastes company money）」。

辦公室情境例句：

The new employee is a <u>clocksucker</u>. He takes an entire day to complete a small task.

新來的那個員工沒效率又白領薪水，他竟花上一整天來處理這麼一件小事。

從另一個角度來看這類型的員工，也不完全都是在混水摸魚，但若要他們「多工作個幾小時，有些人就會急著要求加倍的報酬（someone who works more hours to make the boss happy but really just wants more money）」。

有趣的是，clocksucker也可以用在日常生活的英語，說某人真是「浪費時間、毫無進展」。

約會交往情境例句：

　　After two years of dating, he didn't propose. She said, "You are such a clocksucker!"

　　交往了兩年，他遲遲未求婚。於是她說道：「你真是浪費我的時間！」

　　在雇主（employer）眼中，你被歸類成哪種員工（employee）呢？有沒有遇過上述這兩種類型的人，讓你又愛又恨呢？

　　還有一種同事，遇到事情就擺爛，對於要負責任的情況能避就避，這種員工也是讓人頭痛。「擺爛」的人，英語是這樣說的：avoider。由動詞 avoid（避開、避免）所衍生出來。

Clockless Worker:
Clock in and Clock out, That Matters!
打卡不打卡？有差！

你有沒有這樣的經驗：朝九晚五上班族（nine-to-five worker），每天早上趕著打卡進公司（clock in）；傍晚再盼望著快快打卡下班（clock out）。可以彈性安排上班時間的人，英語怎麼說呢？有些上班族雖然不用待在辦公室加班，卻得把工作帶回家，多花晚上的時間繼續做白天沒做完的事。這樣的工作文化，英語又該怎麼說？本文帶你了解「彈性工時員工」和「下班回家後繼續工作」的英語口語講法！

越來越多老闆或公司讓員工有自願的彈性上班時間。既然不用打卡上下班（clock in / clock out），英語便直接將clock字尾再加上less，就有了clock-less worker一詞：「彈性工時員工」。

情境例句

"As a graphic designer, I can work anywhere and anytime with my laptop. It's fruitless to trap me in the office when I'm running out of creativity. However, the downside of being a <u>clockless worker</u> is missing the bustle of my office. I'm usually out of sync with my coworkers because of my odd hours."

「身為一個平面設計師，我隨時隨地都可用我的筆電工作。若是在我創造力薄弱之時硬要把我留在辦公室，也只是反效果。然而，彈性工時也有缺點，我想念辦公室裡有人氣的忙碌氣氛。因為我的特殊工作時間，我常常都和同事進公司的時間錯開。」

或許有些上班族會羨慕clockless workers在工時上享有的自由，但彈性工時者或許也想感受一下所謂的office politics（辦公室政治），和同事多點時間相處喔！

　　很多上班族可能對以下的內容並不陌生：下班時間到，不是整理好包包就可以輕鬆打卡離開，而是要把一些工作也帶回家。英語裡用extend（延伸）來描述「下班後繼續工作（day-extender）」。

　　當然，大家都不希望得當週末加班的員工（weekend-extender）！

情境例句

"<u>Day-extenders</u> might have to spend one to two hours working at home in the evenings. Sometimes, they may even become <u>weekend-extenders</u>!"

　　「回家後繼續工作的人，每天晚上下班後，可能得撥出一到兩小時來工作。甚至還有可能連週末都在家裡加班！」

　　上班打卡不打卡？真的有差！

上班族英語小常識

　　不管打卡不打卡，大家最怕的還是「超時工作」型的加班方式：work overtime。

e.g. I've been <u>working overtime</u> over the past few weeks, and I hope everything will be worth it.

例句 過去這幾週我都在加班，希望到時一切都值得。

Cyberslacking to Pass the Time at Work?

辦公時間還上網打混？

當員工的人總忍不住在辦公時間上網摸魚嗎？做老闆的會討厭員工掛在網路上打混嗎？讀到這裡，讓你會心一笑了嗎？本篇文章帶讀者用英語觀點來看看在辦公室裡「上網摸魚」的英語俚語（slang）說法和例句用法。

Cyberslackers, be careful!
Bosses hate <u>cyberslacking</u> to pass the time at work!

掛在網路上打混的人小心了！老闆最討厭上班時間還上網摸魚！

情境對話

Ashlee: Here are some ways <u>to pass the time</u> at work!

Barry: You'd better be careful. Our boss hates cyberslacking.

Ashlee: Slacking? I wasn't slacking. I'm usually working my head off. But sometimes, I just have urgent personal business using the Internet.

Barry: But it's still company time and company money. It could get you fired!

Ashlee: Oh, I hope you're not <u>exaggerating</u>.

Ashlee：我有些上班殺時間的方法喔！
Barry：你最好小心點，我們老闆最討厭有人上網摸魚了。

Ashlee：摸魚？我哪有摸魚？通常我都是認真的工作打拼。只是有時候會有些
　　　　緊急的私事要上網嘛。

Barry：但還是用到公司的時間和錢。可能會害你炒魷魚的！

Ashlee：噢！我希望你沒有說得太誇張。

焦點英語

· **cyberslack [s'aɪbə-sl'æk] (v.)**　上網打混

結合cyberspace（網路空間）和slack（偷懶、怠惰、鬆懈）的英語俚語（slang）。

cyberslacker (n.) 指在辦公室時間做與工作無關之上網的員工。

e.g. Cyberslacking prevails among office workers.

例句 上班族盛行電腦上網打混。

· **to pass the time**　殺時間、消磨時光

e.g. He always brings a few books along to pass the time on the flight.

例句 他總會帶個幾本書在飛機上打發時間。

· **exaggerate [ɪgz'ædʒə-ˌet] (v.)**　誇大、誇張、言過其實

e.g. I'm pretty much sure he's exaggerating!

例句 我非常確定他說得太誇張了！

衍生網路用語

　　霸凌的英語是bully，那麼網路霸凌呢？cyber violence：網路暴力、
網路霸凌。

　　網路上的言論自由，提供了人們更多表達意見的管道，尤其是網友們
的匿名留言，近幾年已出現幾件留言失控造成言語傷害、毀謗、人身攻擊
而導致被霸凌者自殺的新聞事件。

Deal with Your Lazy Co-workers!

同事愛偷懶嗎？你可以這樣應付！

本篇文章帶讀者用英語思維來面對打混偷懶的同事，並參考Stever Robbins，這位訓練美國高階主管的教練所傳授的秘訣。

It's not uncommon to come across a lazy co-worker, and they are not always easy to deal with! Carping and tattling won't get you anywhere, but there are a few things you can do to alleviate the issue.

職場上很容易遇到懶惰的同事，甚至，他們還不好應付呢！打小報告或說閒話對你沒實質上的幫助。不過，倒是可以做幾件事來減輕困擾。

Here are 11 tips for dealing with the lazy co-worker from Stever Robbins, a top executive coach graduated from MIT and Harvard Business School.

面對偷懶的同事，擁有麻省理工和哈佛商學院學歷的美國頂尖高階主管教練Stever Robbins建議以下11項處理的方式：

· Don't let them distract you.
別因為他們而讓自己分心。

· Don't get caught up in the issue of fairness.
別執著於公平不公平的問題。

· Don't let it affect your attitude.

別因為他們而影響自己的態度。

· Don't <u>tattle</u>.

不要大嘴巴。

· Don't let their ways rub off on you.

別跟著偷懶起來。

· Don't let your work become your responsibility.

別把他們的工作變成你的責任。

· Don't let them affect your success.

勿讓他們影響你成功。

· Use the opportunity to become the leader.

利用此機會好好認真，晉升領導階層。

· Don't gossip or complain to other colleagues.

別跟其他同事八卦或抱怨。

· Communicate with your co-worker.

和那位同事溝通。

· Don't say yes to projects that require your co-worker to work at full capacity.

不答應接手需要（偷懶的）同事百分百能力的專案。

· **tattle ['tætəl] (v.)**　告狀、打小報告

Urban Dictionary 的解釋：one who reports the wrong doings of others to an authority（向權威者報告他人錯誤的人），請見衍生口語用詞例句。

衍生口語用詞

· **tattle tale**　大嘴巴

> e.g. She is such a <u>tattle tale</u> that always tells the boss when I cyber-slack during the office hours just to pass the time.

> 例句 她真的很大嘴巴！每次我上班時間一上網打發時間，她就跟老闆打小報告。

· **goof off**　摸魚

比cyber slack更混水摸魚的片語講法。

> e.g. That new employee really knows how to <u>goof off</u>, I hope he's not getting kicked out soon.

> 例句 那個新來的員工真的很會打混耶，希望他不會太快被踢走。

Six Lines
Your Boss Should Never Cross

老闆太超過了？6個指標幫你判斷老闆是否踰矩

辦公室裡上司的要求讓你頭痛嗎？還是老闆有踰矩的行為、越過了公事的界線（cross the line）？富比世（Forbes）雜誌上刊載了一篇檢測上司、老闆是否對於下屬有踰矩、越職行為的文章，本文節錄其重點內容，帶讀者邊學英語、也能懂得判別並拒絕太超過的老闆。

If your boss's comments or actions make you feel consistently uncomfortable, then there's a good chance that he or she is <u>stepping over the line</u> of professionalism into <u>inappropriate</u> behavior!

老闆的言行舉止有任何讓你一再困擾的嗎？那她／他極可能對你做出超過專業範圍的踰矩行為了！

If your boss has done one or more of these things with regularity, then it's time to speak up.

如果你的老闆經常有以下的行為，那麼是時候為自己挺身而出了。

· Your boss makes references to your salary in front of other staff.
  你的老闆在其他同事面前提起你的薪水。

· Your boss reprimands you in front of other employees.
  你的老闆在其他員工面前非難、懲處你。

· Your boss has unreasonable expectations.
  你的老闆對你有不合理的期待。

· Your boss shares too many personal details.

老闆跟你分享了太多他自己的私事。

· Your boss makes inappropriate references.

老闆對你有失禮且不恰當的評論。

· Your boss implies that sex, race, age or religion is a factor in work performance.

老闆暗示你的性別、種族、年齡、甚至信仰會影響到你的工作表現。

焦點英語

· **to step over the line**　超過界線、踰矩

同義詞cross the line

e.g. The security guy's really <u>stepping over the line</u> by asking me too many personal questions.

例句 這位保全問了我太多個人問題，實在是太越界了。

· **inappropriate [ˌɪnəˈpropriɪt] (adj.)**　不妥、不恰當、不適當、不相稱的

反義詞appropriate [əˈpropriɪt] (adj.) 適切的

e.g. Talking about salary details is definitely <u>inappropriate</u> at any social occasions.

例句 在任何社交場合談論薪水細節都是相當不妥的。

職稱英語小常識

　　employee（n. 員工、職員）和本文也有出現的staff為同義詞，但staff為不可數名詞。

　　英語中ee結尾的名詞為「被動人稱」的概念，反之，er結尾的名詞有「主動」的意思，例如employer就是雇主。

Running a Meeting:
Ways Back to the Subject

適時插話？表達觀點？你可以把英語說得更自在

常需要用到英語對談的上班族，不免會面對何時該插話、何時得表達想法的窘境。本文帶大家來看看幾種商業場合（business occasion）對談時，表達觀點、適時插話、詢問對方意思與意見等的英語用法。讓你應對進退之間把英語說得更有自信！

表達觀點老實說

· To be honest, ... / Frankly speaking, ...
老實說……／坦白說……

· Let me give you my honest opinion.
老實告訴你我的意見。

· My concern is...
我的考量是……

· I am of the opinion that...
我的看法是……

適時插話、詢問對方意思

· Sorry to interrupt you. Does that mean...?
對不起，打斷一下，這意思是……？

· Excuse me, what does that mean? / What do you mean?

抱歉，您的意思是……？

· I'm sorry to interrupt you. Is that to say...? / Did that mean I have to...?

很抱歉打斷你，這是説必須得……？

· Excuse me, could you be more specific? I don't think I get your point.

抱歉，可以請你説具體一點嗎？我不太懂您的意思。

詢問對方意見

· Do you have any idea?

你有任何想法嗎？

· What's your opinion?

你的意見呢？

· Do you have any thoughts on this?

你對這件事有任何想法嗎？

· What do you think about this? / What do you think? /
How do you feel about this?

你認為如何？

Are You Always Multitasking?
Time to Zero Task!

分身乏術？是時候放慢步調了！

步調總是快速的現代社會裡，時間管理（time management）極為重要，一切都取決於辦事的效率。本篇文章帶讀者來看看兩種截然不同的工作步調。

multitask 同時做好幾件事情的工作方式

multi（多重）和task（任務、工作）所組成的用語。意思是「同時、一口氣做好幾件事情（doing more than one thing at once）」。

上班時，習慣一口氣開啟好幾個視窗和檔案；午休時邊寫個備忘錄或小紙條；總是覺得有很多事情要處理；回到家後邊看電視邊摺衣服；睡前閱讀激勵小品。上述的情形讓你覺得很熟悉嗎？那你完全符合multitasking的工作習性了！來看看以下例句：

· I was late for work, so I had to <u>multitask</u>.
今天上班遲到，導致我得同時處理好幾件事。

· I've been busy <u>multitasking</u> a lot in the office!
我在辦公室裡都忙得分身乏術了！

· He thought he would <u>multitask</u> by doing the physics homework during his math class. His <u>multitasking</u>, however, got him a detention instead.

他自以為可以在數學課堂上做物理作業，這樣的不專心卻反而讓他被留校查看。

zero task 什麼都不做、放慢步調

　　相對於multitask，zero task則是「放手休息、什麼工作都先不做、放慢步調」的意思。來看看以下的情境對話：

Steve: What's your plan for the Chinese New Year?

Eva: Nothing. It's time to <u>zero task</u>.

Steve: I've never heard you talk that way. You're always so on the ball and multitasking.

Eva: Well, if I don't <u>zero task</u> for a change, I'll get sick.

Steve：你農曆過年有什麼計畫嗎？

Eva：沒有。是時候該放慢步調了。

Steve：我從來沒聽你說過這種話。你總是可以積極地同時做很多事。

Eva：這個嘛，如果我不放慢步調、改變一下，我會生病。

Chapter 5

Technology and Innovations
科技革新

Digital Security:
Are You Keeping Your Personal
Data Safe on the Cloud?

安全上雲端？網路個資安全英語用語

日漸普及的雲端資料儲存，該如何小心使用？本文介紹網路個資安全英語用語，並補充新聞時事的英語關鍵字。

How safe is the Cloud after celebrities' photos got <u>hacked</u>?

在（好萊塢）名人的私密照片被駭客外洩後，雲端資料是否安全？

It's one of the biggest celebrity <u>hackings</u>. More than 100 celebrities' nude photos were leaked.

這宗大規模的名人照片被駭事件裡，超過100位明星的裸照被散播出去。

In the new world of cloud computing, digital security is so critical that it can make or break a company. According to Forbes, 61% organizations say that data theft and <u>cyber crime</u> are the biggest threats to their reputation.

在雲端世界裡，數位科技的安全與否，攸關一個公司的成敗。根據美國富比世雜誌今年夏天的報導，61%的企業組織表示，資料偷竊和網路犯罪是他們面臨對公司名譽最大的威脅。

Here are some tips to promote the security in a Cloud (whether you're using iCloud, Google, OneDrive or Dropbox):

下面幾個小步驟，讓你加強雲端資料安全度（不管你使用的是iCloud、Google、OneDrive或Dropbox）：

· Use secure, unique passwords on your accounts and devices.
使用安全、特殊的密碼來開啟你的帳戶和（雲端）裝置。

· Use two-factor authentication when available.
可行的話，使用雙重步驟的身分認證。

· Enable locks and passwords on computers and phone accounts.
在你的電腦和手機帳號啟動上鎖和密碼的功能。

· Run the latest version of an operating system.
採用最新版本的作業系統。

Those steps alone won't ensure that your data can always be safe, but it will minimize how attackers can access your accounts.

這些步驟之一都無法保證你的資料從此安全無虞，不過確定可降低你帳戶被駭的可能。

網路駭客英語小常識

hack (v.) 原本的意思為「切砍、揮砍」，開始有網路資料偷竊後，引申為大家熟知的資料被「駭」。「駭客」一詞就是加上er型的hacker。而資料被「駭」的事情，則用ing名詞型的hacking。正式一點的相關用字為「網路犯罪」：cyber crime。

Spam or Scam?

擺脫垃圾信件：email英語用語

垃圾信件讓人心煩？網路詐騙怎麼說？本文以情境對話幫助讀者更了解 email「垃圾信件」、「刪除信件」、「網路詐騙」等相關英語用語。

Samuel: I couldn't <u>find</u> your email, not even in my trash box. I might have already deleted your email by accident. Can you please email it to me again?

Peggy: Are you sure that the email didn't end up in your <u>spam</u> folder? That happens sometimes.

Samuel: Spam is really <u>getting on my nerves</u>. I was about to delete everything, spam and all.

Peggy: No problem, I'll send it again.

Samuel: Thank you Peggy.

Samuel：我怎樣都找不到你寄給我的信，連垃圾桶裡都沒有。恐怕被我不小心誤刪了。可以請你再寄一次給我嗎？

Peggy：你確定沒把它當作垃圾信件給誤刪了吧？有時候會這樣。

Samuel：垃圾郵件實在讓人受不了。我差點把整個信件匣，垃圾信和其他所有東西都給清空了。

Peggy：不要緊，我再寄一次。

Samuel：謝謝囉Peggy！

· **spam [spæm] (v.) (n.)**　灌水、大量轉貼、或廣告性質的垃圾信

類似用法還有junk posts。

spam還是餐飲英語中的「罐頭火腿」。

e.g. There is this person who always sends <u>spam</u> emails to me, so I have blocked him.

例句 有個人一直寄大量轉寄的垃圾信給我，我只好封鎖他了。

· **get on one's nerves**　太過分、令人抓狂、受不了

也可用out of control（失控）。

over（介係詞）字面上的意思是「超過」，但前面若加上get，便成為動詞片語get over（克服、熬過、釋懷）。

e.g. The construction noise downstairs is annoying and is really starting to <u>get on my nerves</u>.

例句 樓下施工的噪音真的很煩人，我快要抓狂了。

衍生用語

· **scam [skæm] (v.) (n.)**　騙局、詐騙、詭計

　con artist (n.)　詐騙份子

　e.g. Be careful with these <u>con artists</u>! Their <u>scam</u> emails contain links to sell fake medicine.

　例句 小心這些騙子！他們的詐騙電子郵件含有賣假藥的連結。

· **retrieve [rɪ'triv] (v.)**　找回獵物、取回、挽回、重新找回

　忘記email等密碼時，retrieve就是「重新找回、取得」。retrieve原本的意思還有「檢索」和獵犬「啣回獵物」，例如黃金獵犬便是直譯英語gold retriever。比較：find (v.) 只能用在單純找尋失物或一個全新的東西。但要「重新」找回原本就有的密碼，必須用retrieve才合邏輯。

　e.g. His attempt to <u>retrieve</u> his password was unsuccessful, so he had to try again with another email account.

　例句 他嘗試重新取得密碼但卻失敗。只好重新用另外一個電子信箱帳號再試一次。

The Era of Smart Phones:
Apps That Makes Your Life Easier
智慧型手機新紀元：Apps讓你生活更輕鬆

智慧型手機問世後，加上網路的普及，人們越來越依賴手機下載的應用程式（applications，簡稱apps）。先不論一直滑手機用apps這現象好壞與否，有些apps的確讓生活大小事更輕鬆方便、更能與世界接軌。本文介紹四個英語世界裡受歡迎的apps，帶讀者學習相關英語詞彙。

People <u>are obsessed with</u> apps nowadays. Believe it or not, some apps can make your everyday life easier. They can be good helpers by making life more efficient in all spheres. Check out some of the free apps that many people view them as the must-have.

現代人沉迷手機應用程式。不管你相信與否，有些應用程式的確讓你日常生活更輕鬆。為了讓生活更有效率，許多apps可以是很好的幫助。下列幾個是在2014-2015年間，英語世界裡受歡迎、免費、並被大部份人評為必備的apps。

• **Strides**

Strides helps you track your goals and eliminate your bad habits in one place, with flexible reminders and charts to keep you motivated.

Strides幫忙記錄你的目標，並一起除去你的壞習慣。搭配可彈性調整的提醒事項和表格，讓你更有動力。

• First Aid by American Red Cross

Life is full of unexpected surprises. This app provides you the simple step-by-step instructions to guide your through everyday first aid. You can also call 911 at night right from the app in the States.

生活裡充滿了不可預期的「驚喜」。這款app提供你簡易步驟，來處理日常生活裡的醫護急救。人在美國的話，甚至可半夜直接透過此app撥打911求救。

• Pocket Expense Personal Finance

This app brings all your financial accounts together, categorizes your transactions, tracks all your bills, lets you set budgets and helps you achieve your savings goals.

這款app一口氣整理你所有的銀行帳戶。把每筆交易明細分類、記錄帳單、編列預算，並幫助你達成存錢目標。

• Relax Melodies

For those who want to improve health, this app features relaxing sounds that help you fight stress and fall asleep faster. You can select the sounds, such as ocean waves and winds in the trees, and combine them to create a mix.

對於想改善健康的人，這個app以紓緩的聲音幫助你對抗壓力，並讓你更容易入睡。你可選擇喜歡的聲音，例如海浪聲或樹梢的風聲，並自行混音。

焦點英語

・**obsessed [əb'sɛsd] (adj.)**　對……著迷、沉迷的

用法：be + obsessed + with + (n.) / ving

e.g. He's so <u>obsessed with</u> his new smart phone that he used it too much to get some good sleep.

例句 他整個迷上他新的智慧型手機了，結果手機玩太多都沒好好睡覺。

・**stride [straɪd] (v.) (n.)**　邁步、大跨步、快馬加鞭、驅策

引申意思：使人有動力、動機、行動力。

e.g. He managed to keep his <u>stride</u> on this project while making decisions.

例句 他試圖在這個案子上保持做決策的行動力。

手機版英語字典app下載小常識

　　智慧型手機（smart phones）和網路普及的年代，以下列出兩項筆者在大學和留學機構授課時，推薦學生下載的app字典，不管是iOS或Android系統都找得到：

・Merriam-Webster：台灣坊間說的「韋氏大字典」。這個英英字典幫助你學習道地的美式英語字彙。字彙學習小提醒：加強英語字彙，一定要從英語例句來學習，別只看中文字面上的解釋喔。英漢字典的中文定義，都只能當作片段翻譯的參考。還是要從例句裡理解，才不會用中文思維去想英語字，不小心用出「台式英語」。

・Urban Dictionary：每一個字彙都搭配對話式例句，讓你更清楚生字使用的情境。查生字的同時，連會話練習都顧到了。這個字典還特別針對口說英語、文化用語、雙關語等做加強。也有每日精選生字，讓你學到英語的流行語。

Technology Designs VS. Fashion Sense: Google Glass

Google Glass：當科技遇上時尚設計

Google在2013年推出的Google Glass，打著結合時尚與科技創意設計的賣點，還未正式上市就已製造了話題！不讓蘋果的設計專美於前，現在各界都在引頸期盼屆時的市場反應。本文帶讀者一窺Google Glass。

進入本文前，請先想想以下詞彙的英語怎麼說：

A. 網路創業公司

B. 幕後花絮

C. 普及運算（電腦運算中，強調和環境融為一體的計算概念）

答案就在本文中！

　　As Google and other companies begin to build wearable technology like glasses and watches, an industry not known for its fashion sense is facing a new challenge: how to be stylish. Design has always been important to technology with products like Apple's becoming fashion statements, but designing hardware that people will wear like jewelry is an entirely different task.

　　正當Google也把科技跨足時尚之際，可穿戴的科技產品如眼鏡、手錶等，正順勢而起，這樣的時尚潮流也讓科技業面臨了前所未有的市場挑戰：怎樣的產品才有型有款？設計一直都是科技產業重要的一環，特別是在這幾年看到蘋果的成功後，消費者關注的還有時尚。不過，首飾類的科技產品對業者來說，又是個新挑戰了。

A computer you wear on your face that looks a bit like eyeglasses, Google Glass lets users take pictures or record video without using their hands, send the images to friends or post them online, see walking directions, search the Web by voice command and view language translations. Google Glass accesses the Internet through Wi-Fi or Bluetooth linked to the wireless service on a user's cell phone. And users activate Glass by speaking, touching the frame, or moving their heads.

看起來像是戴著眼鏡，實際上卻是台電腦，這就是Google Glass！戴上Google Glass後，不需動手就可以聲控操作照相、攝影、上傳影像分享給朋友、看道路指南、搜尋網頁、讀取語言翻譯等。Google這隻眼鏡只要憑藉用戶手機的無線網路分享或藍芽就可以上網。甚至，只要聲控、碰觸鏡框或轉轉頭就可以啟動Google Glass。

"Changing behavior is much more challenging than changing technology," said Olof Schybergson, founder and chief executive of Fjord, a design company that has helped clients build wearable devices. In sign of how acute the challenge is for Google, the company is negotiating with Warby Parker, an **(A)e-commerce start-up company** that sells trendy eyeglasses, to help it design more fashionable frames.

「改變行為模式比改變科技還要困難！」Fjord的創辦人兼執行長這樣説。Fjord這間設計公司已幫不少客戶訂製可穿戴的科技產品。有感於即將面臨的市場挑戰，Google正和一家電子商務創業的眼鏡公司洽談中，希望能與其合作，為Google眼鏡設計更多有型又時尚的鏡框。

In addition to considering partnering with Warby Parker, Google is doing other things to recruit the fashion-savvy, particularly women. It could open retail stores where people can try on the glasses. At New York Fashion Week in 2013, models wore colored versions on the runway for Diane von Furstenberg, and the designer made a **(B)behind-the-scenes video** wearing the glasses.

與眼鏡公司合夥的計畫之外，Google也打算招聘具時尚感的女性員工，更計畫像蘋果一樣設立零售店面，讓民眾可以實際試戴眼鏡。在2013年的紐約時裝週上，模特兒們在伸展台上展示了Diane von Furstenberg設計師的彩色鏡框，而設計師本人更是配戴眼鏡錄製了一段幕後花絮。

For Google, the glasses are a major step toward its dream of what is known as **(C)ubiquitous computing (ubicomp)**, the idea that computers and the Internet will be accessible anywhere and we can ask them to do things without lifting a finger. The biggest obstacle now is getting people to use them.

Google眼鏡是Google邁向夢想中普及運算科技的主要一大步。運用普及運算的主要概念是讓人們隨時隨地都可使用電腦和網路，甚至不需動到你一根手指頭。而現階段最大的挑戰是，怎樣讓大家想用這眼鏡。

焦點英語

· **in sign of**　跡象顯示、表示……

同義詞as a sign of

e.g. He'll take that offer <u>in sign of</u> the fierce competition.

例句 有感於競爭激烈，他將接下這個職務。

· **in addition to**　此外、除了……之外

e.g. <u>In addition to</u> plan A, we'll have to come up with plan B as well.

例句 原本的計畫之外，我們還得再想出一個備用方案。

· **savvy [s'ævi] (n.) (v.) (adj.)**　知道、了解

e.g. She's been around and <u>savvy</u> a lot.

例句 她見多識廣，懂很多。

Chapter 6

Business and Economics
商業經濟

Marketing Lessons:
Four Success Tips

英語行銷術讓你出奇制勝

線上購物與網路行銷（online marketing）當道，本篇文章帶讀者來看看評價最高的網路洋酒購物中心Wine.com總裁Rich Bergsund所建議的4大網路行銷術。

For today's marketers, online channels present a vast array of new opportunities. Here are the four tips on building a successful, <u>sustainable</u> campaign online.

對今日的行銷人來説，網路通路呈現了廣大且成列的新商機。以下提供Wine.com總裁Rich Bergsund所建議的網路行銷4招，幫助你建構成功且永續經營的網路推銷手法。

· Build your base: a strong customer base.
建構行銷基礎：確保主要客源。

Before diving right into the latest, hottest marketing trend and investing in emerging channels, it's critical to build a strong customer base.

在你投入和投資最新最熱門的市場趨勢前，先建立穩固的基礎客源是關鍵。

- **Watch the trends before diving in.**
  投入資金前先觀察市場流行趨勢。

  Major trends, like smart phone use, carry direct impact over the way consumers shop and engage.

  以市場的流行趨勢來舉例：像是智慧型手機的使用，這個趨勢大大影響了消費者的消費行為和投入。

- **Make sure you're listening and aggregate feedback.**
  確保你有聆聽顧客需求，並總集顧客反應。

  When developing strategies to amplify reach, remember: Your customers will tell you what to do, you just have to make sure you're listening.

  發展行銷策略擴大範圍時，切記：你的顧客會告訴你該怎麼做，你只需確定你有聆聽客戶需求就好。

- **Deliver.**
  表達。

  Listen to what your customers' demand and trust them, as they are the experts. Use the insights to deliver both an excellent product and experience. Aim to delight customers so much they can't help but return and bring friends.

  聆聽並信賴顧客需求，要相信顧客絕對是專家。好好利用這點去傳達最佳的商品和服務經驗。行銷目標要放在取悅客戶，讓他們樂於帶著朋友一起回購。

· **sustainable [səst'enəbəl] (adj.)**　可持續發展的、永續經營的

e.g. Economic expansion must be <u>sustainable</u>, so that a large number of people can benefit from it.

例句 經濟成長應當是持續的，這樣才能讓大多數人都得益。

永續經營英語生活小常識

　　已經盛行了多年的「樂活」（LOHAS，lifestyle of health and sustainability），就是崇尚「健康」（health）和讓環境「永續經營保存」（sustainability）的生活方式。

Wildposting, Where the Ads Go Wild

廣告宣傳太失控？相關英語詞彙

大都會裡，公共空間常張貼了滿滿的廣告，有時甚至似乎要把建築物也蓋過了！本篇文章乃根據作者在紐約街頭的經驗，帶讀者學習街道上廣告看板、電子看板等英語說法，搭配情境對話，一窺廣告瘋狂張貼的現象。

**Wildposting has taken over the street
scenes in metropolitans.
And it does not stop where the city ends.**

大量的廣告張貼佔據了都會街景。

而且，這樣瘋狂的張貼並不僅止於城市裡面。

上面例句明明在講廣告，但卻看不到ads（advertisements）一字？首先來學習這個口語單字：由wild（adj. 野的、瘋狂的）和posting（n. 廣告或公佈等張貼）組合而成的新詞：wildposting（失控的廣告宣傳）。

來看看以下幾類會出現在十字路口、街道上、公路上和大眾運輸交通工具上面的分類廣告，英語怎麼說：

· billboards and banners 廣告看板和旗幟

Peggy: Turn here! You missed the turn!

John: Where's the turn? I didn't see it.

Peggy: It's behind the billboard.

John: I didn't see it because of the billboards and banners along the highways. All these wildpostings are blocking the traffic signs.

Peggy：在這邊轉彎！你錯過了！
John：哪裡說要轉彎？我沒看到！
Peggy：就在廣告看板後面啊！
John：就是因為整條公路上的廣告看板和旗子，我根本就看不到嘛！這些瘋狂
的廣告張貼擋住了交通號誌！

**· flashing texts and moving icons on electrical billboards
電子廣告看板上閃爍的文字和跑馬燈圖片**

John: At intersections, <u>electrical</u> billboards compete with traffic controls. The flashing <u>texts and</u> moving <u>icons</u> are everywhere!

Peggy: Oh well, it's visual competition.

John: Yes, and sometimes businesses even get their employees to dress up as some giant dolls or animals to <u>prance</u> around the street corners.

Peggy: Ha-ha. That's what I call wild.

John：在十字路口，電子廣告看板與紅綠燈一較高下，那些跑馬燈文字和圖片
到處都是！
Peggy：喔！視覺上的競爭嘛！

John：是呀！有時候商家還會要員工穿上玩偶裝，或扮成動物，在街角走來走去引人注意。

Peggy：哈哈！這樣打廣告就真的瘋狂了！

・TV commercials 電視廣告

電視上播放的廣告，英語用commercials，不同於（平面）分類廣告的advertisements。

焦點英語

・**electrical [ɪl'ɛktrɪkəl] (adj.)** 　電子的、帶電的

不同於electronic（adj. 電器的），加上s變成名詞electronics（電器用品）。

e.g. He works as an <u>electrical</u> technician here.

例句 他在這裡的工作是電工技師。

・**texts and icons** 　分類廣告、簡訊、郵件中的「文字和圖片」

e.g. Some designers choose <u>icons</u> rather than <u>texts</u> simply because icons take up less space.

例句 有些設計師選擇圖片而非文字（做廣告），單純因為圖片佔據的版面較小。

・**prance [pr'æns] (v.)** 　昂首闊步、大搖大擺、招搖的走路

是語意較誇張的動詞。

e.g. The little girl <u>prances</u> around the house in her new clothes.

例句 小女孩穿著新衣開心地在家裡到處走。

The Lifestyle Choices of LCE and LFFE

低碳經濟，怎麼做怎麼說？

環保又符合經濟效益的生活方式，已是環保團體和各國政府積極提倡的節能做法（save energy）。本文帶讀者來學習相關英語辭彙和例句。

地球暖化現象（global warming）日趨嚴重，使人們更加意識到環境的議題，這樣的環保意識也反應在經濟發展。為了緩解溫室效應（the Green House Effect）和人類各項活動造成的二氧化碳排放量（carbon emission），環保人士大力提倡「低碳經濟」的生活形態：LCE(low carbon economy) and LFFE(low fossil-fuel economy)，希望業界和政府都能鼓勵「低碳發展」（low carbon development），並開發「低碳技術」（low carbon technology）。

以下是相關英語辭彙和例句，一起瞭解幾種「低碳生活」的範例：

• efficient light bulbs 節能省電燈泡

別看到efficient（效率高的），就翻譯成「效率高的燈泡」喔！efficient bulbs就是現在越來越普及的「省電燈泡」，也可以說成更口語的energy-saving bulbs。

e.g. We shall replace our old light bulbs with efficient ones. <u>Efficient light bulbs</u> save lots of energy. They use only about one-third of the power of normal ones.

來把我們的舊燈泡換成節能省電的吧！這種燈泡省下的電量可觀，耗電量只有普通燈泡的3分之1。

·carbon footprint 碳足跡

凡走過必留下痕跡。但這邊講的足跡（footprint），可不只是腳印喔！在環保議題上，「碳足跡」這概念是用來計量人類從事各項日常活動所產生的「碳排放量」（carbon emission）。就連觀光旅遊業者也越來越常提到，其旅遊形態有意識到碳排放量，並採用低排放量的旅遊形態供民眾遊憩。美國環境保護局（EPA, US Environmental Protection Agency）網站提供了一個線上計算機，讓民眾檢測日常生活各活動的碳排放量（例如搭乘交通工具的選擇和里程數），透過確切的數據讓大家反思如何減少二氧化碳的排放，不使溫室效應和全球暖化氣候變遷（climate change）繼續惡化。

EPA 碳排放量計算機：http://www.epa.gov/climatechange/emissions/ind_calculator.html

e.g. Everyone should be aware of Green House Gas (GHG) emissions caused by organizations, events and products. The way we live leaves a carbon footprint, affecting every other human, our fellow creatures and the earth we cohabit.

例句 每個人都該去留意各組織、活動和產品所造成的溫室效應氣體排放。我們生活的方式會留下碳足跡，並影響其他人、生物，以及我們共同居住的地球。

• eco bag 環保購物袋

可重複使用的環保購物袋，也可以說reusable shopping bag。各大國際精品早已相繼推出環保袋來彰顯他們重視環境議題的態度。血拼之餘，也別忘了少製造不必要的塑膠購物袋，對我們的環境友善點喔！（eco-friendly）

e.g. Eco bags are a more eco-friendly alternative than the regular plastic ones because they can be reused.

例句 與傳統塑膠袋相比，環保購物袋這種可以重複使用的新型態對環境友善多了。

低碳經濟衍生用語＋環保英語小常識

alternative energy 新興能源

經濟發展上，避不開能源（energy）的議題，為了減少碳排放量，並解決舊有能源短缺的問題，許多新興能源的產業早已興起。新興能源（alternative energy）也可說成綠能（green energy）或可再生能源（renewable energy），都是緩解溫室效應和全球暖化的做法。以下列出許多國家（包括台灣）都在大力開發的alternative energies：

· solar panel 太陽能面板

· wind turbine 風力（渦輪）發電機

· hybrid car 油電混合車

All Retailers Want for Christmas is Big Data

零售商最想要收到的聖誕禮物：大數據

社群網站中被關注和按讚的內容，還有網路關鍵字的搜尋次數以及網頁瀏覽人次，這些數據（big data）都蘊藏了龐大的商機。

美國感恩節過後開始的折扣季，網路購物的零售也頗讓人注目，不讓百貨公司、實體購物中心、暢貨中心的打折專美於前，而這現象也帶出了一個事實：網路上的數據資料提供了零售業者極大的商機來源（business intelligence），也是商人在折扣季開始前或推出產品前，最想要得到的耶誕禮物。

閱讀本文前，請先想想以下詞彙的英語怎麼說：

A. 黑色星期五

B. 商務E化

C. 用智慧型手機瀏覽網路購物商品

答案就在本文中！

It is reported that 57 million Americans shopped online on **(A)Black Friday**, a 26% increase over 2011. As retailers <u>settle in</u> for this, their biggest selling season of the year, the use of big data has become a critical force in growing sales. Big data analytics is helping retailers stay in front of a new breed of consumer, the omni-channel shopper, and the avalanche of data they are generating. This transformation is in large part driven by advances in mobile, digital, social media and location-based technology. Consumers are shopping across multiple channels from stores to catalogs, online websites and mobile devices.

　　據報導，2012年有5,700萬美國人在黑色星期五（感恩節後的第一個星期五，美國折扣季打折最多的第一天）上網血拼，而網路購物的人數較2011年增加了26%。這樣的網購趨勢，讓各家零售商在美國冬季大折扣時，不得不投入網路戰場，同時，擁有大量的線上客戶資料，更成為銷售量成長與否的決勝關鍵。大數據的分析，幫助零售商得以應付全面購物管道的消費者和如雪崩般襲來的客戶數據。這樣的消費結構轉型和以下科技息息相關：可攜式的數位社群媒體和定位科技。消費者因此得以透過多種途徑購物：實體店面、商品型錄、網站、行動裝置。

With its ability to foster a sales experience that <u>melds</u> the advantages of physical stores with the information-rich experience of online shopping, it's not surprising that consumers and retailers alike are eager to embrace omni-channeling retailing. Savvy retailers and **(B)e-commerce** companies have turned to big data analytics during the crucial holiday shopping season to increase sales, better target customers, improve reach and keep a competitive advantage. They are using big data to analyze tweets, reviews and Facebook likes, and matching this data against customer lists, transactions, and loyalty club memberships to determine online promotional campaigns.

看見了實體店面的實際銷售優勢和網路購物的豐富資訊，消費者和零售商都懂得要合併這兩者的優點，迎接全通路的購物時代。特別在假日的購物季，精明的零售商和商務Ｅ化的公司，都轉向網路上的龐大數據來增加銷售、鎖定客戶族群、改善並維護其銷售上的競爭優勢。生意人利用線上的數據來分析社群網站（如推特、臉書）的評論內容和按讚的數目，再以此找出符合特定族群的客戶名單、交易、忠誠的會員，來決定如何宣傳其網路銷售。

　　Here are some industry examples that illustrate the future of retailing and big data: 1. Tracking the omni-channel supply chain. 2. Distilling better intelligence from customer data. 3. Generating real-time pricing from big data algorithms. 4. Connecting one-on-one with shoppers. 5. <u>Countering</u> **(C)smart phone "showrooming"**.

　　網購趨勢點出了數據如何影響零售的未來，來看看下面幾則業界利用客戶線上數據的例子：1. 追蹤全通路的商品供應鏈。2. 從客戶相關數據中萃取商機。3. 從數據的計算中整合出實際的銷售金額。4. 和購物者一對一接觸。5. 順勢和智慧型手機瀏覽網購的趨勢接軌。

焦點英語

· **settle in** 　安頓、進入、適應新環境

　　`e.g.` It is not so easy to <u>settle in</u> a new country.

　　`例句` 在新的國家安頓下來不太容易。

· **meld [m'ɛld] (v.)** 　合併、混合

　　`e.g.` We tried to <u>meld</u> my plan with her marketing strategy.

　　`例句` 我們嘗試把我的計畫和她的行銷策略結合。

· **counter [k'aʊntɚ] (v.)** 回應、反駁、（提早、搶先一步）反應

e.g. The chairperson tried to persuade him into this, but he did not counter.

例句 主席試了說服他，他卻不回應。

　　實體店面利用民眾放假，在感恩節隔天的 **Black Friday** 大促銷，抓準大量民眾開始有空血拼、採買聖誕或新年禮品。猶如我們的週年慶，在打折第一天折扣最多，衝衝買氣。除了 **Black Friday**，感恩節4天連假後的週一（每年11月的第4個星期四為感恩節，加上週五和週末連放4天），更是商人用在網路商店的折扣日，近年網路購物盛行，也因此衍生出了感恩節後的週一網購折扣日：cyber Monday。

Business Quotes from Movies

人生如戲：經典電影台詞點出商場道理

> 許多經典電影，永存的對白不僅精采睿智，其寓意也足以啟發職場上的應對進退。本文整理出幾部知名電影的經典台詞，讓讀者以英語觀點領略其中商場道理。

閱讀本文前，請先想想以下詞彙的英語怎麼說：

A. 詐騙高手

B. 首腦

C. 股票經紀交易公司

答案就在本文中！

• *Catch Me If You Can* (2002) 神鬼交鋒

True Story of the **(A)con artist** Frank Abagnale Jr. (Leonardo DiCaprio), who collected cash passing himself off as an airline pilot, doctor and lawyer. Quote: "Two little mice fell into a bucket of cream. The first mouse quickly gave up and drowned, but the second mouse, he <u>struggled</u> so hard that he eventually churned that cream into butter and he walked out. Amen." - Frank <u>saying grace</u> before meal

本片為美國詐騙高手Frank Abagnale Jr.（Leonardo DiCaprio；李奧納多狄卡皮歐飾）的真實故事，偽造鈔票並曾順利冒充機師、醫師、律師。經典台詞：「兩隻老鼠掉進了一罐鮮奶油裡，第一支老鼠很快放棄並溺死。第二隻老鼠卻奮力掙扎、再掙扎，以致於鮮奶油被它攪成了奶油塊，最後爬了出來。阿們。」——節錄自Frank於電影裡的某場飯前禱告

• *American Gangster* **(2007) 美國黑幫**

True story of the 1970's heroin **(B)kingpin** Frank Lucas (Denzel Washington) and Richie Roberts (Russell Crowe), the cop seeks to arrest him. Quote: "The loudest one in the room is the weakest one in the room." - Frank Lucas to his cousin Huey

本片為美國1970年代黑幫老大、也是販賣海洛因的首腦Frank Lucas（Denzel Washington；丹佐華盛頓飾）的真實故事，Frank與警察Richie Roberts（Russell Crowe；羅素克洛飾）針鋒相對， Richie一直試圖要將Frank追捕到案。經典台詞：「最大聲的人，也是在場最弱的人。」——節錄自Frank對堂弟所說的台詞

• *Pursuit of Happiness* **(2006) 當幸福來敲門**

Based on a true story of Chris Gardner (Will Smith), a <u>struggling</u> salesman trying to make it as a stockbroker and support his son. Quote: "You got a dream you gotta protect it. People can't do something themselves, they wanna tell you can't do it." - Gardner to his son Christopher (Jaden Smith)

本片根據Chris Gardner（Will Smith；威爾史密斯飾）的真實故事改編而成：力爭上流的推銷員，為了撫養兒子，努力成為股票交易員。經典台詞：「好好保護你的夢想。因為總有人因為自己做不了，而告訴你你也做不到。」——節錄自Gardner片中與兒子（Will Smith親生兒子Jaden Smith飾）的對白

• *The Godfather* (1972) 教父

The definitive mobster movie. Quote: "I'm going to make him an offer he can't refuse." - Don Corleone (Marlon Brando) hinting in which he will convince a film producer

寓意明確的黑幫電影。經典台詞：「我將要提出的條件，會是他無法拒絕的。」──節錄自Don Corleone（Marlon Brando；馬龍白藍度飾）暗示他將會說服一位電影製片

• *Boiler Room* (2000) 搶錢大作戰

Seth Davis (Giovanni Ribisi), <u>lured</u> by the promise of "a million dollars in three years," takes a job at the **(C)brokerage firm**, J.T. Marlin, but soon finds out the true nature of their business. Quote: "A sale is made on every call you make. Either you sell the client some stock or he sells you a reason he can't. Either way a sale is made, the only question is who is gonna close?" - Jim Young (Ben Affleck) in a sales-training session

Seth Davis（Giovanni Ribisi；喬凡尼瑞比西飾）被「3年100萬美金」的承諾所引誘，任職於馬林股票經紀公司，但不久後就發現這門生意的真面目。經典台詞：「每筆交易都靠你每通電話。不是你賣出了股票給客戶，就是對方告訴你他不買的原因。不管是上述哪一個，都是一筆成了定局的交易。唯一的問題是，誰要拿下這筆交易？」──節錄自Jim Young（Ben Affleck；班艾佛列克飾）在電影裡的銷售訓練課程

· **say grace** 禱告（通常指飯前的謝飯禱告）

grace ['gres] (n.) 恩典

e.g. Son, can you <u>say grace</u> for us?

例句 兒子，來幫我們做飯前禱告吧？

· **struggle ['strə-gəl] (v.)** 掙扎、拼命、奮力於某事

e.g. Ever since dropping out of school, he has been <u>struggling</u> his way out to the position nowadays.

例句 自從休學後，他就一路拼命到今天這個位子。

· **lure ['lur] (v.)** 引誘、誘捕、誘使、誘導、誘惑 **(n.)** 誘餌

e.g. The politician finally responded to the scandal by saying that he was <u>lured</u> from the very beginning.

例句 這位政治人物終於對其醜聞有所回應，聲稱他在最開始就被引誘了。

Chapter 7

News Report and Current Issues
新聞報導與當代議題

USD$300 from the Airport?!
Taxi Fare around the World
全世界最貴的計程車機場接駁在哪裡？

若你是經常出差往返世界各地的商務人士，計程車似乎是從機場到市區最方便的交通方式。你知道全世界最貴的機場計程車接駁在哪裡嗎？2014年的全球統計顯示了各大城市機場的平均計程車車資，讓你下回出發到這些城市前，在交通預算上有心理準備。

進入本文前，請先想想以下詞彙的英語怎麼說：

A. 計程車車資

B. 外匯

C.（幣值）貶值

答案就在本文中！

Arriving at an airport and jumping into a taxi is the preferred option for most, and a necessary expense for time-pressed business travelers. But trying passing off a $300 airport to city center **(A)taxi fare** and your account department may like to have a chat with you when you return to office.

抵達某地機場後跳上計程車，這似乎是大部分旅客偏好的交通方式，尤其在出差趕時間時，也是必要的開銷。不過300美金的車資從機場到市區，等你出差回國後，辦公室的會計部門可能會想找你談談。

$300 taxi fare? That's how much the average cab ride from Tokyo's Narita airport into the city center costs, making it the world's most expensive, according to a new survey by British **(B)foreign exchange** company, Moneycorp. <u>By comparison</u> a single ticket on the Narita Express train to the heart of Tokyo costs $28.

300美金的計程車費？從日本成田機場到市中心差不多就是這個價錢！根據英國一間外匯公司（Moneycorp）的最新調查，日本成田機場往東京市區的計程車費高居全球之冠，這樣的高車資，相對於成田機場快線單程票美金28元的票價，的確是天價。

Tokyo's main international airport is 66 kilometers (41 miles) from the city, explaining a large part of the expense. <u>Despite</u> a **(C)weakening currency**, making the journey almost 10% cheaper than at the same time last year, Japan remains an expensive destination for many visitors.

東京最主要的國際機場距離市中心有66公里（41英哩）之遠，或許這解釋了高價計程車車資的原因。儘管日幣的跌幅讓這段機場到市區的計程車車資略比去年低了約10%，日本還是位居全球最貴的機場計程車接駁之首。

Geneva in Switzerland is the next most expensive fare per kilometer. The Norwegian capital and Italian city cost visitors $112 and $106 <u>respectively</u> to reach the city center. Visitors will have to budget in high transfer costs. Both cities are over 40 kilometers from the airports.

若以每公里車資換算的話，日內瓦的機場計程車是第二高價。前往挪威和義大利首都的旅客也要分配多點交通預算了，這兩國的機場市區計程車車資分別是美金112元和106元，兩國機場都距離市區至少40公里之遠。

Learn how much each airport to city center taxi fare costs:

來看看下面幾個國際機場的計程車平均車資：

City / Airport 城市／機場	From the airport to the city center 機場—市中心距離	Average taxi cost 平均單趟計程車車資 （機場—市中心）
Newark （紐約）紐華克	26 km	$62
San Francisco 舊金山	21 km	$44
Hong Kong 香港	34 km	$30
Beijing 北京	25 km	$22
Bangkok 曼谷	30 km	$8.50
Delhi 德里	16 km	$4
Melbourne 墨爾本	23 km	$57
Paris Charles de Gaulle 巴黎戴高樂	23 km	$57
Lisbon 里斯本	9 km	$21
Amsterdam 阿姆斯特丹	18 km	$53
Geneva 日內瓦	8 km	$33

· **by comparison (adv.)** （與……）相較、比較起來

e.g. By comparison, trips during the winter break usually cost the visitors more because of the peak season.

例句 相較之下，因為寒假是出遊旺季，會花費旅客較多的旅費。

· **despite [dɪsp'aɪt] (prep.)** 儘管

e.g. Despite a shortage of steel, the industrial output has been growing.

例句 儘管鋼鐵短缺，工業產量仍然持續成長中。

· **respectively [rɪ'spɛktɪvli] (adv.)** 分別、各自……

e.g. In the speech contest, Lisa and Stacy won first and third respectively.

例句 這次的演講比賽，Lisa和Stacy個分別得到第一名和第三名。

Ice Bucket Challenge Blows Up Social Media: Social Awareness for ALS

社群媒體慈善熱潮：看冰桶挑戰如何澆醒公益

2014年夏天流行的「冰桶挑戰」，截至2015年8月為止越燒越熱，透過以Facebook為主的社群媒體，成功喚起大眾對於「漸凍人」的關懷與認識。本文以英語觀點藉此活動，帶讀者學習「熱潮、流行」的幾個英語名詞和動詞片語。

The Ice Bucket Challenge <u>went viral</u> on social media this summer. This challenge is a big gift for the ALS Association: The organization raised more than US$10 million on August 21, 2015 alone.

今年夏天，「冰桶挑戰」在社群媒體上像病毒擴散一樣，迅速流行起來。這對美國肌萎縮性脊髓側索硬化症協會來說是個大禮：光是2015年8月21日單日的募款就突破美金1000萬元。

What is ALS (Amyotrophic Lateral Sclerosis)?

什麼是肌萎縮性脊髓側索硬化症（俗稱漸凍人）？

Amyotrophic lateral sclerosis is a neurodegenerative disease with various causes. It is characterized by muscle spasticity, due to muscle atrophy, and difficulty in speaking, swallowing and breathing.

肌萎縮性脊髓側索硬化症是一種神經漸漸退化的疾病，成因有許多。發病徵兆有：肌肉萎縮造成的癱瘓、說話與呼吸吞嚥困難。

In mid-2014, the Ice Bucket Challenge <u>blew up</u> social media and became a <u>pop culture phenomenon</u>, particularly in the United States, with numerous celebrities, politicians, athletes and everyday people posting videos of themselves online.

　　2014年中，「冰桶挑戰」在社群媒體上發燒，迅速成為以美國本土為主的大眾文化現象，不少名人、政治人物、運動明星，還有一般人都張貼影片到網路上。

Before the challenge, public awareness of ALS was relatively limited. The ALS Association state that by the time of the Ice Bucket Challenge going viral, only half of Americans had heard of the disease.

　　在這股熱潮之前，對於漸凍人的大眾意識還相對有限。美國肌萎縮性脊髓側索硬化症協會表示，在冰桶挑戰流行前，只有一半美國人聽過此病。

As long as there's the Internet, any <u>trends</u> could occasionally go viral. However, the ALS Ice Bucket Challenge isn't going away. Even if you think the whole <u>fad</u> is stupid or dangerous to pour ice water all over yourself, it's still important to awake the public awareness and to donate to ALS. Visit the ALS Association homepage and click the donate bottom on the right: http://www.alsa.org/

只要有網路的一天，任何風潮都可能突然間傳開。不過冰桶挑戰還沒結束，即使你可能覺得這股全身淋冰水的熱潮很蠢、很危險，重要的是，能夠喚醒大眾意識，並捐款予美國肌萎縮性脊髓側索硬化症協會。進入美國肌萎縮性脊髓側索硬化症協會網站首頁，點選頁面右上角的「捐款」：http://www.alsa.org/

很多廣告行銷手法，在網路年代得仰賴社群媒體的經營與曝光。本文提到了兩個動詞片語，就是表達「流行現象」的英語辭彙：

· go viral 消息散播開、流行開來

· blow up 吹起……的風潮、激起……的流行意識

而流行現象不外呼和pop culture phenomenon（大眾文化現象）、trend（風潮、流行、趨勢）、fad（一時的熱潮）有關。

After Hurricane Sandy, Businesses Try to Keep Moving

颶風過後，重振商機

2012秋天遭遇颶風橫掃的美國東岸，在歷經了接連幾天停電和淹水的窘境後，各方投資者都在觀察市場恢復狀況，而業界和電力公司也盡一切所能，恢復正常上班、供電。作者以當年風災期間在美國對新聞親身的觀察，帶讀者以英語閱讀當年颶風過後的美東狀況，並探討天災後的經濟復甦措施。

進入本文前，請先想想以下詞彙的英語怎麼說：

A.（天災）肆虐

B. 遠距工作

C. 煉油廠

答案就在本文中！

Businesses across a broad **(A)swath** of the East Coast struggled to recover from Hurricane Sandy, even as executives <u>conceded</u> that it would be days, at least, before things returned to normal.

整個美東在歷經了Hurricane Sandy風災肆虐後，正從困境中掙扎著復甦市場景氣。不過，就連政府部門執行長都不得不承認，至少要花少好幾天，才能讓各行各業恢復正常。

In New York City, banks and other financial services firms predicted that they would be mostly <u>back on their feet</u> when financial markets reopened and customers began to venture out to local branches.

就紐約市來説，在金融市場重開市後，銀行和金融機構便可回復正常營運，而原本的客戶將可開始出資至國內分行。

JPMorgan Chase's headquarters on Park Avenue and its principal trading floors a few blocks north on Madison Avenue are set to reopen, as are at least 100 hub bank branches in New York, New jersey and Connecticut that were stocked with extra cash before the storm. About 25,000 employees at JPMorgan Chase **(B)worked remotely** on the first Monday after Hurricane Sandy, but that figure dropped to 15,000 to 20,000 on the next day as lights went out across the region.

風災前就備好多餘現金的摩根大通，在紐約、紐澤西、康乃迪克有至少100家分行。其位於紐約市公園大道上的總部和總部附近麥迪遜大道上的投資大樓，都已準備好重新開市。約25,000名摩根大通員工在颶風過後的週一遠距工作，但隨著隔日大停電，能夠遠距上班的員工數量跌至15,000到20,000之間。

For many companies, as for individuals, the big question mark was when power providers and other utilities would be functioning reliably again. More than five million households in New York, New Jersey and Connecticut were without power on the first Tuesday after the storm.

對許多公司行號來說，此次風災後最大的問題是，供電和其他水電設備能否再次穩定運作。在紐約、紐澤西、和康乃迪克，超過500萬戶在颶風過後的週二開始停電。

Some retailers rushed to reopen stores and stock them with everything from extra batteries to mops and cleaning supplies. Fuel providers seemed to have escaped the worst of Hurricane Sandy's wrath. As technicians returned to some idled **(C)refineries**, their early reports suggested that regional gasoline and fuel supplies would not be seriously affected by the storm.

颶風剛走，一些零售商就趕著開店，貨品架上備滿電池、拖把等民生必需品和清潔用品。其他像是石油供應商，看起來似乎是在這次風災過後的困境中逃過一劫。正當技術員在趕回閒置的煉油廠之際，報告顯示美東區域的石油和瓦斯供應不會受颶風太大影響。

All told, the lost <u>output</u> from and overall effects of the storm could shave as much as 0.6 percentage points off annualized fourth-quarter economic growth, according to an analysis by IHS Global Insight.

一如大家所知，這場颶風造成了些許經濟產量損失。根據環球透視的分析，風災使這4分之1年度的經濟成長削減了0.6%。

· **concede [kəns'id] (v.)**　讓步、（不情願、不得不）承認

e.g. Are you willing to <u>concede</u> the right to us?

例句 你願意把權利讓給我們嗎？

· **back on one's feet**　恢復、重新振作

e.g. The divorce cost him a fortune took him three years to get <u>back on his feet</u>.

例句 離婚讓他花了一大筆錢，更花了他3年時間才重新振作起來。

· **output ['aʊtpˌʊt] (n.)**　（經濟）出口、產量

e.g. The <u>output</u> of his factory this year has increased by 15 percent as compared with last year.

例句 他工廠今年的產量較去年增加了15%。

Starbucks Introduces USD$1 Reusable Cup to <u>Cut Down on</u> Waste

售價僅美金1元！星巴克推出可重複使用的飲料杯：少浪費、愛地球

地球暖化（global warming）越趨嚴重，聯合國最新調查顯示，碳排放量已達新高，環保意識高漲之下，各企業界有責任付諸行動愛地球。本文報導星巴克美國總部新推出的環保杯，下回點咖啡喝時別忘了對環境盡一份心力！

進入本文前，請先想想以下詞彙的英語怎麼說：

A. 可重複使用的

B. 直營連鎖店

C. 交叉感染

答案就在本文中！

Starting on January 10, 2013, Starbucks customers will have the option to save their planet and their wallets, a dime at a time. The coffee giant is offering USD$1 plastic cups, which can be used for drink purchases at a discount of ten cents.

從2013年1月10號開始，到星巴克消費時，多了一個既環保又省荷包的選項來拯救我們的地球。這間全球知名咖啡連鎖店，新推出美金1元、可重複使用的塑膠杯，讓消費者買飲料時省下美金10分。

The director of environmental affairs at Starbucks stated that while the company has sold **(A)reusable** tumblers for some time and offered the ten cent discount, he expects that the modest price of its new one, available at **(B)company-owned stores** in the U.S. and Canada, will encourage consumers to take action more frequently. The new effort comes largely in response to consumer criticism over the volume of paper coffee cup waste, approximately 4 billion cups globally each year, generated by Starbucks.

星巴克的環境事務執行長表示，可重複使用的星巴克隨行杯已銷售了一段時間，並提供9折優惠給使用隨行杯的顧客。星巴克預計先在美國、加拿大直營門市推出低價環保杯，鼓勵消費者更常使用。這樣的舉動是為了回應顧客所批評的紙張浪費問題：全球每年約消耗掉40億個星巴克紙杯。

According to a 2011 report issued by Starbucks, that year, customers used personal tumblers more than 34 million times, nearly 2% of all beverages served in global company-owned stores. While this represented a 55% increase in personal tumbler use from 2008's tally, Starbucks admitted to challenges in tracking cup use both in and away from their stores.

根據星巴克的2011年度報告，星巴克消費者在2011年，使用隨行杯的次數超過34,000,000次，佔了全球星巴克直營店飲料總銷售數的2%。這份報告更顯示，相較於2008年，2011年星巴克隨行杯的使用量增加了55%。星巴克更同意接下這份挑戰：追蹤內用和外帶的環保杯使用量。

The reusable cups are made in China, and have fill lines inside denoting "tall," "grande" and "venti" sized drinks. The cups will be rinsed with boiling water by Starbucks employees before they're refilled, reducing the risk of **(C)cross-contamination**, but at least one more challenge remains: will customers actually remember to bring them into the store?

這款中國製的環保杯，內有容量刻度，標示飲料屬於中杯、大杯、或特大杯。每回重複使用前，星巴克員工都會用滾水沖洗過，排除交互感染的風險。但即使如此，新推出的飲料杯仍面臨以下挑戰：顧客真的會記得把杯子帶回咖啡店嗎？

The question is, could you remember to bring along a reusable cup each time? Here are the feedbacks from the customers: "I've got a mug on my person at all times." "It might be tricky, but the savings are worth it." "I'd probably forget and would end up buying at least a few." "I'd bring it once or twice and forget." "I'm not even going to bother trying."

問題來了，你會記得隨身帶著這環保杯嗎？看看以下星巴克顧客的回應：「我都隨時攜帶自己的馬克杯。」「這有點麻煩，但可以省錢的話就蠻值得的。」「我應該會忘記帶出門，最後又重複買了幾個環保杯。」「我可能會記得一次或兩次，然後又忘記帶。」「我才懶得試這種環保杯。」

焦點英語

· **cut down on (v.)** 削減、減少

同義詞reduce [rɪ'djus]

e.g. People who cut down on added sugars in their diets can lose weight effectively.

例句 減少飲食中糖分的攝取可讓人有效減重。

· **at all times (adv.)** 隨時（都……）、無論何時、一直

同義詞anytime ['ɛnɪ͵taɪm]

片語比較：all the time = always (adv.) 總是

e.g. Your family is supportive at all times.

例句 家人一直都會支持你！

otorcar in the early 20th century. Railway companies in Europe and the United States used streamlined tra
33 for high-speed services with an average speed of up to 130 km/h (80 mph) and a top speed of more than
0 mph). The first high-speed train was the Italian ETR 200 that in July 1939 went from Milan to Florence at
th a top speed of 203 km/h. With this service, these trains were able to compete with the upcoming airplanes
a Odakyu Electric Railway in Greater Tokyo launched its Romancecar 3000 SSE. This set a world record
auge trains at 145 km/h (90 mph), giving Japanese designers confidence that they could safely build even fa

Chapter 8

Resume Skills and Job Interview
履歷求職大作戰

8-1 **Get Your Resume Ready!**
履歷求職大作戰！

8-2 **Four Tips to Avoid Resume Black Hole**
避免履歷石沉大海：你可以這樣做

8-3 **7 Things You Can Do After a Bad Job Interview**
面試不成功嗎？7招讓你反敗為勝！

8-4 **5 Mistakes College Job Seekers Make**
新鮮人求職，這5件事請小心！

8-5 **World Top Employers for New Grads**
全球百大企業要什麼？英語思維看業界職缺

8-6 **13 Things Mentally Strong People Don't Do**
心智強大法則：快樂職涯的13個要訣

8-7 **Emotional Intelligence to Get You There!**
高EQ讓你更成功！

Get Your Resume Ready!

履歷求職大作戰！

職場新鮮人正準備要出社會找工作嗎？還是你最近有轉職或另覓新出路的打算？本文帶讀者用英語觀點來看看撰寫履歷時，要注意的版面內容、應避免的字、以及該小心提及的工作經歷。

If you're applying for a job recently, make sure every word on your resume page should be working hard to highlight your talents and professional skills.

若你近期正在找工作，寫履歷時要確定一件事：放上去的每一個字句都該能夠充分表現你的才華和專業技能。

Tips for composing your resume: Be specific.

撰寫履歷的小秘訣：具體描述。

The top of your resume matters a lot for the <u>career objective</u>, and it needs to grab the hiring manager's attention with a list of your top accomplishments.

針對你所應徵的職稱，履歷上半部的內容是最大關鍵：優先在上半部放上夠亮眼的表現來吸引主管的青睞。

在撰寫非公司所提供的制式履歷時，career objective（應徵職務）應緊接著放於個人聯絡資料下的版面。其後再放針對此應徵職務的相關工作經歷。

　　履歷項目撰寫順序如下：

· personal information (with the highest education)
　個人聯絡資訊（包含最高學歷）

· career objective 應徵職稱

· experiences 經歷

· references available upon request
　應公司要求所附的參考資料

Resume

Lily Thompson

lily12345@123mail.com

0987654321

Current address: 347 Green Street, Concord, NH03301

Job Objective

Sales Manager

Highest Education

Bachelor in Business Management

Southern New Hampshire University

Certificates & Skills

TOEIC Certificate, score 900   08/2012

Work Experience

Sales Manager, W&W Real Estate   09/2013-present
- Supervise and manage a sales staff of 5
- Conduct and provide direction to meet project targets

Sales Representative, TR Insurance   10/2011-09/2013
- Analyzed the specific needs of customers via surveys to develop data
- Increased profits by 10% in two years

It's much more effective to list some actual results of your experience that portray your good qualities in action than to simply claim you have them by using vague adjectives.

最有效的履歷寫法是，（用英語動詞）條列出你工作經驗中實際的成果。因為這些實際的職場經驗才是凸顯你個人強項的關鍵。避免用形容詞描述工作經歷和成果。

在列出實際成果（actual results）時，盡量使用「動態動詞（action verbs）」，英語動詞若能用conduct（執行）就不要用assist（協助）；用lead（帶領）取代hold（舉辦）；用accomplish（完成、成就）取代present（呈現）。

Four Tips
to Avoid Resume Black Hole
避免履歷石沉大海：你可以這樣做

投出履歷後就只能空等待嗎？該如何避免履歷寄出後沒有回音？本文統整美國職涯規劃網站的觀點，帶讀者用英語觀點學習，提醒自己在撰寫履歷時要注意的版面內容，以及寄出履歷後該做什麼事。

Human resource people and hiring managers receive tons of resumes for any job opening, and they would end up missing, skipping, or tossing a lot of them.

通常開出一個職缺後，人力資源和負責招募的主管會收到難以計數的履歷，但主管們有可能最後會搞丟、略過不看、或直接丟掉一些履歷。

Experts and consultants suggest the tips for avoiding resume black hole:

（求職）專家和顧問提供了避免履歷（寄出後）石沉大海的秘訣：

- **Have someone proofread your resume.**
  請人幫你檢查履歷內容。

Before sending your resume, have at least one person you trust review it so that it can have a better chance of catching the eye of the employer.

寄出履歷前，至少請一個你信任的人幫你再看一遍，檢查過後的內容更有可能獲得主管的青睞。

- **Keep it simple.**
  保持版面簡單。

Avoid graphics, logos and any other things that may clog how the employers read your resume.

避免圖像、標誌,或任何會阻礙求職主管閱讀履歷的版面內容。

- **Research the company's hiring process.**
  (事先)研究該公司的招募過程。

Do they look first at your qualifications or experiences? Doing research helps you properly prepare to avoid the black hole.

公司會先看符合條件?還是資歷?做點研究幫你避免把履歷投入了黑洞。

- **Network into the company and use your connections.**
  運用人脈,直接交涉該公司。

Let your networking contact know that you're applying for a position and try to determine who the hiring manager is and send a resume directly to that person with a letter asking for an informational interview.

讓你在業界的人脈知道你正應徵某職缺,並試圖知道招募的主管是誰,直接寄出履歷給對方,並附上要求面試機會的信件給此主管。

7 Things You Can Do After a Bad Job Interview

面試不成功嗎？7招讓你反敗為勝！

　　別讓不成功的面試經驗影響你。本文是作者長期閱讀美國業界雜誌後，搭配實際輔導應屆畢業生英語面試和履歷撰寫技巧的經驗，帶讀者以英語觀點看看大部份企業主管的建議，學習面試後該怎麼做，讓你從不成功的面試經驗中記取教訓、並在之後的工作應試中反敗為勝！

A "bad interview" can mean a lot of things; the candidates believes <u>retrospectively</u> that he or she <u>flopped</u> on a majority of the questions, he or she didn't adequately prepare for the interview, the candidate is dressed inappropriately, says something offensive or arrives late, or a personal issue - like a family death or a break-up - distracts the candidate during the interview, among other things.

　　「不成功的面試」可能包含了下面的情況：應試者不斷回顧不愉快的面試過程，並認為自己沒有好好回答面試時的主要問題；面試前沒有做好充足準備；面試穿著不恰當；言詞激怒了面試主管；遲到等等。也可能是一些私事讓面試者分心，而影響了面試的情緒，例如：親人過世或是和另一半分手。

7 things you can do after a really bad interview:

　　面試不順利嗎？7招教你這樣做：

· Reflect from the experience.

　　從經驗中反省。

176

· Learn from it.

從錯誤中學習。

· Learn to forgive yourself.

學習原諒自己。

· Explain what went wrong in a follow-up thank you note.

面試後，在寄給面試主管的致謝信中，解釋自己表現失常的原因。

· Use the thank you note to add anything you might have forgotten to mention during the interview.

在致謝信中補充說明自己面試時忘了講的部份。

· Inform the employer of any outside distractions.

告知面試主管讓自己分心的重大私事。

· Never apologize for a bad interview, but do say sorry for specific slip-ups.

千萬別為了面試表現不好而道歉。但一定要為自己的失言說聲抱歉。

焦點英語

· **retrospectively [rˌɛtrospˈɛktɪvli] (adv.)**　回顧、追溯地

英語解釋：Looking back on or directed to the past.

e.g. Retrospectively, I feel a little bit embarrassed.

例句 回想起來，我感到有點尷尬。

· **flop [flˈɑp] (v.)**　重物猛然落下、失敗

e.g. If somebody is flopped, they are beaten up.

例句 （口語英語中）若說某人flopped，等同於beaten up（被打敗）的意思。

5 Mistakes College Job Seekers Make

社會新鮮人求職，這5件事請小心！

又到了社會新鮮人的求職季節！初出校園，準備好履歷和就業目標了嗎？美國2013年的春季調查中，統計出求職新鮮人易犯的錯誤和應有的態度。本篇文章帶讀者用英語思維，注意求職時要小心的地方！

A new study in the States shows that college students need to be doing a lot more to set themselves up for a job after college!

美國一篇最新研究顯示，應屆畢業大學生面臨求職時，還沒做的努力，其實比他們以為的要多更多！

According to the report, conducted by a career website After-College from a March survey, most college students did not <u>result in</u> a job offer because of the five mistakes the students are making.

根據美國知名職涯網站「AfterCollege」針對求職大學生的調查，大部分還沒應徵到工作的學生，是因為犯了5個錯誤。

The consultancy <u>in conjunction with</u> AfterCollege ticked of the five mistakes:

配合「AfterCollege」進行調查的顧問公司，挑出了這5項錯誤：

- **Students are not applying for enough jobs.**
  應徵的工作不夠多。

College students should go after 30-40 job offers at once. It's like your full time job to get a job now!

應屆大學畢業生應該一口氣應徵30到40個職缺。要有這種態度：「找工作」就是你現在的全職工作！

- **Failing to do enough of their networking.**
  沒有建立足夠的人脈管道。

Ask your school's career office for opportunity / help!

從學校的職涯中心尋求機會和協助！

- **Spending time on Facebook and YouTube when they should be using LinkedIn.**
  應該上LinkedIn建立個人檔案，卻花時間在Facebook和YouTube上。

  Create your LinkedIn profile to promote yourself!

  快上LinkedIn建構你的求職個人檔案！

- **Believing that applying through an employer's website is all they need to do.**
  以為直接上各個公司的網站申請工作就好了。

  Make a good use of social networking sites like LinkedIn!

  善用LinkedIn等社群網路！

- **Taking "no" for an answer when you get no response from an employer.**
  投出履歷後若沒得到回應，就以為被拒。

  Don't give up! Contact your college career office, your personal network of family and friends, LinkedIn and Facebook to find a personal connection!

  別就此放棄！聯絡大學裡的職涯辦公室、親朋好友、各個社群網路，取得個人聯繫管道！

RESUME

CAREER SUMMARY

18 years in civil design and construction. Early experier
structural designer in consulting firm specializing in hi
commercial building and cement plant then shifting to
and gas industry. Currently assigned as Civil Superviso
ongoing project Greenfield Area.

Familiar with ACI, AISC, ASCE, UBC, BS DEP , AASH
NSCP Standards

Familiar with ASME, API, ANSI, TEMA, BS, Shell DEP
and NEMA Standards

焦點英語

- **result in**　導致、發生……的後果

  e.g. The budget mistakes <u>result in</u> a damage to the profits.

  例句 預算上的錯誤會導致公司利潤的損失。

- **in conjunction with**　與……一道、協力、配合

  e.g. He runs this business <u>in conjunction with</u> his siblings.

  例句 他和兄弟姊妹一起經營這份事業。

World Top Employers for New <u>Grads</u>

全球百大企業要什麼？英語思維看業界職缺

美國新聞媒體CNN旗下的CNNMoney，調查了全球大學生最想進入的企業，本文節錄3間年輕人嚮往的大公司，搭配徵才主管對於應屆畢業大學生和社會新鮮人的公開建議，帶讀者以英語思維了解各知名企業所要招募的人才。

What are the following world top employers looking for?

下面幾家全球知名企業，要找什麼樣的人才？

• **Microsoft 微軟**

To impress recruiters, show you're someone who "lives the lifestyle of a <u>geek</u>, besides being a geek in the classroom," the Microsoft recruiter advises. "So join those hacker groups at campus and work on tech <u>start-ups</u> if you can." "Every six months commit yourself to doing something that will help you grow outside of the classroom," says Microsoft recruiter Anthony Rotoli.

「要獲得青睞，你得『活得像個天才怪胎，而不是只在課堂上當書呆子。』在校園裡就加入駭客等電腦社團，可能的話，甚至著手進行科技創業。每6個月就投入一項事物，讓自己能在教室外有確實的成長。」微軟徵才主管如此建議。

- **KPMG 畢馬威會計師事務所**

Half of KPMG's full-time hires come through its internship program, says the executive director of campus recruiting. Recruiters look for candidates with global experience (i.e., from studying a career-relevant topic abroad) as well as extracurricular activities that demonstrate leadership savvy.

KPMG校園徵才的執行主管表示，近一半正職員工來自於實習部門。所要招募的人才得有國際觀（例如：有和求職領域相關的國外求學經驗），並有課外活動經驗來展現領袖氣質。

- **Apple 蘋果**

Recruiters are looking for perfectionists, idealists and inventors, according to its careers site. Apple values people who are passionate about every detail and constantly searching for ways to make things better.

根據蘋果的求職網站，徵才人員正在尋找完美主義者、理想主義者和發明家。對於細節擁有熱情、並持續追求卓越的人，是蘋果看重的人才。

· **grad [græd] (n.)** （大學／應屆）畢業生

口語英語中有許多拼字的縮減，graduate（大學畢業生）縮寫為grad即是一例。

應屆畢業生：recent graduate。

e.g. That recent <u>grad</u> has been working his part time as an intern here since last summer.

例句 那位應屆畢業生從去年夏天開始就在這邊打工實習了。

· **geek [gik] (n.)** 書呆子

類似用字：nerd。科技業常自嘲其員工都來自天才型的書呆子與宅男。甚至微軟（Microsoft）美國西雅圖（Seattle）的總部（Microsoft Campus），在紀念品販賣中心還銷售印有geek字樣的各式紀念品。

e.g. Some might laugh at those engineers as <u>geeks</u>, but the truth is you can't deny they are really talented.

例句 或許有些人會笑這幾個工程師是宅宅的書呆子，但不可否認的是，他們真的蠻有才的。

· **start-up** 創業

動詞片語「start up (a business or a company)」的名詞用法。

e.g. This company grew from a small <u>start-up</u> to multimillion-dollar corporation.

例句 這間公司從小型創業成長為百萬美元的大企業。

13 Things Mentally Strong People Don't Do

心智強大法則：快樂職涯的13個要訣

職場上面臨壓力和挑戰在所難免，該如何調整以適應？本文例舉幾個要訣，引導讀者用英語思維培養健康的心靈。

We have to admit that mentally strong people tend to lead a better career path. Staying mentally healthy is actually trainable by exercising positive minds. Let's read how mentally strong people keep up the good vibes.

我們都必須承認，心智健康的人較容易發展出更好的職涯。保持心智健康實際上是可以靠著正面思維訓練出來的。來看看心智強大者如何維持好的氣場（good vibes）。

- **They don't waste time feeling sorry for themselves.**
  不浪費時間在對自己感到抱歉或遺憾。

Take responsibility for your role in life and understand that life isn't always easy or fair.

對自己生活裡扮演的角色負起責任，人生並非都一帆風順。

- **They are not afraid to change.**
  不怯於改變。

- **They don't waste energy on things they can't control.**
  不把精力浪費在無法控制的事物上。

  The only thing you can control is your attitude!

  你唯一可以控制的是自己的態度！

- **They don't give away their power.**
  不隨意給人（控制自己的）權力。

  They don't allow others to control them. For example, they don't say things like, "My boss makes me feel bad," because they understand they're in control of their emotions.

  不讓他人控制自己。舉例來說，別說：「我老闆讓我覺得很糟！」這樣的話，因為自己的情緒該由自己控制。

- **They don't worry about pleasing everyone.**
  不擔憂如何去討好每個人。

  Speak up or say no when necessary.

  必要時勇敢發言或直接說不。

- **They don't fear taking calculated risks.**
  不害怕（承擔）計算過輕重的風險。

- **They don't <u>dwell on</u> the past.**
不沉溺於過往。

They acknowledge their past, live for the present and plan for the future.

心智強大的人會承認過往、把握當下、計劃未來。

- **They don't make the mistakes over and over.**
不重複犯同樣的錯。

- **They don't <u>resent</u> other people's success.**
對他人的成功不感到眼紅。

Mentally healthy people can appreciate and celebrate others' success.

心智健康的人能夠欣賞並祝福他人的成功。

- **They don't give up after the first failure.**
不因一次失敗就放棄。

- **They don't fear being alone.**
不怕獨處。

They aren't afraid to be alone with their thoughts, and they can use this <u>downtime</u> to be productive.

別害怕面對獨處時的思緒，利用這樣的休息期讓自己重新整頓、再有一番作為。

- **They don't feel the world owes them anything.**
不要覺得全世界都欠你。

- **They don't expect immediate results.**
不求立即的回報。

· **dwell [dw'εl] (v.)** 　停留、棲息、居住在⋯⋯

引申意思：沉溺於某種狀態或環境，搭配介係詞on。

e.g. Old people often <u>dwell on</u> the passing days.

例句 老人家常喜歡緬懷過往。

· **resent [riz'εnt] (v.)** 　憎恨、厭惡、感到眼紅、心生怨恨

e.g. Paradoxically, the less you have to do the more you may <u>resent</u> the work that does come your way.

例句 矛盾的是，你該做的工作越少，你就越可能憎恨落在你手頭上的事。

· **downtime [d'αʊnt,αɪm] (n.) [UC]**

（工廠等）停工期、停機、（營業場所）歇業期 【不可數名詞】

e.g. This problem can damage material and create unnecessary <u>downtime</u> and extra cost.

例句 這個問題會造成材料受損，並製造不必要的停機和額外的成本。

衍生用語

　　口語英語中的ups and downs（起起伏伏），用來表示生活中有高有低，並非都一路順遂。

e.g. Life does not always show you the bed of roses, and you have to accept all the <u>ups and downs</u>. What's more, when life gives you a lemon, make it the lemonade!

例句 人生不會總是美麗、一帆風順（英語裡用「bed of roses（玫瑰花床）」來比喻生活中的美好），你必須接受所有的起伏，甚至，當生活丟給你檸檬時，把它榨成檸檬水喝了！

Emotional Intelligence
to Get You There!
高EQ讓你更成功！

> 當努力和聰明才智沒有和職場表現成正比時，到底什麼關鍵因素可以推你一把？本文綜合美國富比世雜誌（Forbes）的報導，佐以科學研究數據，帶讀者以英語觀點來認識情緒商數（EQ），並學習相關用語。

There's an interesting finding: people with the average IQ outperform those with the highest IQ 70% of the time. So what is it to achieve the professional success in addition to the inevitable efforts?

一項有趣的研究發現： 70%的狀況，智商中等的人反而表現的比高智商的人來得好。所以，除了必須的努力之外，到底是什麼帶出職場的成功？

EQ (or Emotional Intelligence) is the critical factor, and it is the essential part of the whole person besides of IQ.

情緒商數（EQ）就是關鍵的因素，在一個人的智商之外，EQ扮演了很重要的一環。

到底EQ在職場上扮演了什麼關鍵角色？和一個人的智商又有什麼不同？看看以下兩段英語：

About 34% executives and managers said they are placing greater emphasis on one's EQ when hiring and promoting employees. There even goes a saying like this, "IQ might get you hired, but EQ get you promoted!"

約34%的主管表示，在徵才與升遷員工時，他們越來越著眼於一個人的EQ。甚至有句話這樣說：「智商使人得以被錄用，而情緒商數使人得以晉升！」

The good news is that, you can increase your EQ by developing one's self-confidence and positive attitudes while IQ is the same at age 15 as well as it is at age 50.

好消息是，藉由培養自信和樂觀的態度，EQ是可以被提升的。智商就不一樣了，一個人15歲時的智商到50歲時還是一樣。

情緒商數英語小常識

EQ (Emotional Intelligence Quotient)
情緒商數，又稱情緒智商（情商）

Studies have shown that people with high EQ have greater mental health, better job performance and more potent leadership skills.

研究指出，高情商的人會有較健康的心理狀態、較好的工作表現、更強的領導能力。

國家圖書館出版品預行編目資料

專欄英語好有趣 / 吳青樺著
-- 初版. -- 臺北市：瑞蘭國際, 2016.04
192面；17×23公分. --（繽紛外語系列；57）
ISBN 978-986-5639-65-5（平裝附光碟片）
1.英語 2.讀本

805.18   105005025

繽紛外語系列 57

專欄英語好有趣
Newspaper Columns with English & Chinese Insights

作者｜吳青樺（Emilia）・責任編輯｜紀珊、王愿琦
校對｜吳青樺、紀珊、王愿琦

內文錄音｜吳青樺、Steven Barton・錄音室｜純粹錄音後製有限公司
封面、版型設計、內文排版｜余佳憓

董事長｜張暖彗・社長兼總編輯｜王愿琦・主編｜葉仲芸
編輯｜潘治婷・編輯｜紀珊・編輯｜林家如・設計部主任｜余佳憓
業務部副理｜楊米琪・業務部專員｜林湲洵・業務部專員｜張毓庭

出版社｜瑞蘭國際有限公司・地址｜台北市大安區安和路一段104號7樓之1
電話｜(02)2700-4625・傳真｜(02)2700-4622・訂購專線｜(02)2700-4625
劃撥帳號｜19914152 瑞蘭國際有限公司・瑞蘭網路書城｜www.genki-japan.com.tw

總經銷｜聯合發行股份有限公司・電話｜(02)2917-8022、2917-8042
傳真｜(02)2915-6275、2915-7212・印刷｜宗祐印刷有限公司
出版日期｜2016年4月初版1刷・定價｜350元・ISBN｜978-986-5639-65-5